THE SNAKE STOMPER

Lean, handsome Kim Logan was a hired gunman—a snake stomper—when he went to work for Peg Cody to protect her Clawhammer Ranch from Hank Dunning's rival outfit. Peg was an attractive, fiery redhead and Kim dreamed of becoming master of Clawhammer.

But trouble was brewing in Pass Creek Valley. And when Hank Dunning started a run on the bank to ruin Peg, Kim tried to save her—only to find himself framed for a murder he didn't commit.

After a desperate jail break, Kim learned that Peg had double-crossed him. Throwing his hand in with the small valley ranchers in their fight for survival against Peg and Dunning, Kim met single handed the most dangerous challenge of his fighting career.

THE SNAKE STOMPER

Joseph Wayne

GUNSMOKE

First published in the UK by Wright and Brown

This hardback edition 2008
by BBC Audiobooks Ltd
by arrangement with
Golden West Literary Agency

ISBN 978 1 405 68184 1

British Library Cataloguing in Publication Data available.

Printed and bound in Great Britain by
Antony Rowe Ltd., Chippenham, Wiltshire

TABLE OF CONTENTS

CHAPTER 1

THE STRANGER

KIM LOGAN followed the pass road to the top, paused for a moment until he saw the coach and six climbing far below him, and went on. No hurry. Plenty of time. This might be a wild goose chase, but still the job had to be thought out. That was a rule of the profession. Think it right down to the finish. The odds weren't so important if you have the edge and hold it. Never pull a gun until you have to, and not then unless you're willing to kill the man you're drawing it on. Never let the idea that the other man might be faster enter your mind.

Professor Kim Logan, M.G. Master of Guncraft. Kim laughed softly as he jogged down the east slope. Why, he could write a book on how to be a tough hand. He had served his apprenticeship on the border with as salty a crew as a man would find. The fact that he was alive at the ripe old age of twenty-five proved his fitness to write the book. He was the only one of the old bunch who could do any writing; the graves of the others were scattered from the Rio to the Dakota badlands.

The summit was above timber line. Now Kim came to the first stunted spruce on the east side of the pass and reined his buckskin off the road. There was a level stretch here just above a sharp pitch where the stage always made a brief stop. He dismounted, shivering a little, for it was cold at this altitude even in August. He rolled a smoke, considering the slowly approaching stage.

This wasn't the sort of job Kim liked. Too many people involved who had no part in the business, and he'd had his doubts from the first that the man he wanted would be on the stage. Besides, Johnny Naylor who was riding shotgun was an unpredictable gent who might decide to be a hero. But when a man was drawing gun wages from a boss like Peg Cody, he didn't question his orders. Not if he liked his job, and Kim liked this job pretty well. There might be a future with Peg and her Clawhammer spread. She was single, pretty, and in need of a man like Kim Logan.

Kim led his horse behind a spine of rock and stepped into the road. The stage rounded a curve below him and came laboring on up the steep grade. Kim eased back around the rock and waited. Minutes later the coach stopped, the driver saying, "You can see for yourself there ain't no trouble. You've been drinking too much coffee. You're getting so damned jumpy you'll be shooting at shadows."

Kim stepped into view, his .44 palmed. "A little trouble, Butch. Take it easy, Johnny."

The driver cursed. Johnny Naylor shouted, "Logan," in a scared voice; his lips quivered and tightened. Jumpy, all right, and dangerous.

"I told you to take it easy, Johnny," Kim said as if this were a casual thing. "You've got a wife. Butch, you've got three kids and a wife. I'd hate like hell to make some widows and orphans today."

"All right, let's see what he wants, Johnny." The driver hunched forward on the high seat, the tip of his tongue moistening his lips. "But I'm telling you one thing, Logan. The sheriff'll trail you to hellangone, and don't figure on Clawhammer being big enough to save your hide."

Kim had had his look at the passengers. His man was here. He said, "You've got a fellow I want. Yuma, step down."

"Kidnapping," Johnny Naylor cried. "You're loco, Logan. The box is plumb heavy. Why ain't you taking it?"

"I ain't a thief. You oughtta know that, Johnny. And Butch, you don't need to say anything to Ed Lane. I'm saving a man's life. Even our chuckle-headed star toter wouldn't jail a man for that. Yuma, I ain't telling you again. Step down."

There were three passengers: a drummer Kim had seen a few times in Ganado, a fat woman with a cartwheel hat who looked as if she was close to fainting, and a little man with a deeply lined face scoured by wind and sun to a dark brown. The little man would be Yuma Bill. He would be tough if pushed too far, Kim judged, and for a moment it was touch and go.

"And who would you be saving my life from?" the little man demanded.

"Some gents you never heard of," Kim answered, "but I'm saving it all right. Take my word for it."

Still Yuma Bill made no move to get out of the coach. His right hand was not in sight. He asked, "What's this Clawhammer you're talking about?"

Kim grinned. He liked a man who had guts. Not the jumpy ones like Johnny Naylor. To Kim's way of thinking, that wasn't guts. His kind died young. But old Yuma Bill was something else. He figured things before he made a play.

"Clawhammer's my outfit," Kim said. "A woman named Peg Cody runs it."

"Don't let that fool you," Johnny Naylor cried. "She's as tough as Logan."

"Clawhammer," Yuma Bill murmured. "Peg Cody. Them names don't mean a damned thing to me."

"Maybe Brit Bonham does," Kim said.

"Yeah," Yuma agreed, "it does." He swung the coach door open and stepped down, a shoe box clutched in his left hand. "Roll 'em, driver. I'll go along with this Logan."

"You're loco . . ." Johnny Naylor began.

"Shut up," the driver shouted, and kicked off the brake, the silk flowed out and cracked with pistol-sharpness, and as the coach lumbered on over the pass, the fat woman quietly fainted.

Yuma Bill held out his hand. "Things must be doing over here in this country. Wilder'n hell, Brit wrote."

"Plenty wild," Kim agreed, gripping the outstretched hand. He nodded at the shoe box. "Got your lunch there?"

For an instant the little man's faded blue eyes narrowed as doubt flowed across his face. He said, "Yeah, my lunch."

"Well, throw it away. We'll pick up a bait of grub on the other side of the pass."

"If you don't mind," Yuma said, "I'll hang onto it."

"Sandwiches for Brit Bonham maybe," Kim murmured, and turned toward the rock ledge.

Yuma followed, and when he saw there was only one horse, he asked, "Figgering on me walking?"

"I'll get a horse for you on the other side of the pass. We'll ride double that far. You never know how a job like this is gonna turn out. I didn't want to leave a horse if I had to make a run for it."

The little man nodded. "Now suppose you tell me what I'm heading into."

"Nothing, I hope. I aim to deliver you personally to Brit Bonham at Ganado along with your lunch. Then you'll hear the stage was held up twice today, and you'll thank me for taking you off."

They mounted, Yuma Bill hanging tightly to his shoe box. He remained silent until they were over the pass and swinging southward through the spruce. Then he said, "I knowed Brit right well when he had a bank in Las Animas, and he was never one to get into trouble."

"They've got law in Las Animas," Kim said. "On Pass Creek a man packs his law on his hip. That leaves Brit in bad shape."

"Who's building a fire under him?"

"Ever hear of a gent named Hank Dunning?" Kim asked. "Or the HD outfit?"

"No."

"You will if you hang around these parts. Takes pretty long steps, Hank does."

9

They rode in silence for a time, dropping fast as they angled southwest. An hour later the trail curled through a stand of aspens, and Kim pulled up at the edge of a slick-rock rim that fell away a sheer hundred feet. The slope directly below was covered with pine, but farther to the west the timber played out. It was a rough country below the pines, sparsely covered by cedars and piñons and broken by ridges reaching finger-like into the valley.

"This rim goes all around the west side of the valley," Kim said, "but you'll get the best look from right here you'll get anywhere along it. That silver ribbon you see winding around down there is Pass Creek. The valley is Pass Creek Valley, and right in the middle you'll see some buildings. That's Ganado, or what's left of it. Used to be a big mining camp, but it's just a cow town now."

Yuma Bill studied the long flat sweep of the valley, made a little hazy now by dust and smoke from some distant forest fire. He asked, "Where's them ranches you were talking about?"

"Clawhammer's on this side, HD's on the other, and both stay on their side of the creek. You can't see the buildings from here."

"A damned big valley for two ranches," Yuma said.

"There's some little outfits scattered around the fringe, but they don't cut much ice."

"You say Clawhammer is run by a woman?"

"That's right." Kim swung his horse back into the trail. "We'll get there, come evening."

"I thought you were taking me to Ganado."

"I didn't say when."

"Damn it, Brit wrote like he was in a hurry for . . ." Yuma Bill stopped, then added, "For me to get there."

"Now maybe he is, but I work for Peg Cody, so I take orders from her. She said to bring you to Clawhammer."

"Why?"

"You'll have to ask her."

Kim felt the sharp pressure of a gun muzzle shoved against his spine. "You're taking orders from me," Yuma Bill said flatly. "We're going to Ganado. Savvy?"

"Sure," Kim said, "but we'll take the long way. Now if that don't suit you, go ahead and blow my backbone in two. Then you'll play hell getting to Ganado. Alive, I mean." He turned his head and gave Yuma Bill a grin. "You won't be real popular around that burg. Not with Hank Dunning anyway. I figure he'll have a reception committee waiting when he hears you weren't on the stage for his boys to pick off."

"All right." Yuma replaced his gun. "Maybe you're hoorawing me. Maybe not, but I'll find out."

10

"One thing I ain't clear on," Kim said. "Your coming to Pass Creek is about as smart as sticking your head into a bear trap. What's it gonna buy you?"

"Not a damned thing," the little man said, "but I'm hoping I can save Brit's hide."

"And get your belly full of lead."

"I'll take that chance. I've owed him something for a long time, and I reckon I'm the only one he could get help from. I couldn't turn him down."

"I'll deliver that shoe box with Brit's sandwiches. You can catch the stage back to Del Norte. Or go on to Durango if you want to."

"I'll see it through to the finish," Yuma said. "In my book a man pays a debt personally."

"My book don't read that way," Kim said.

Yuma Bill let it go at that. The trail followed the rim for half a mile, then swung westward through a break to the pines below. Near noon they reached a small park with a log house and barn and corrals set in the center.

"What's this?" Yuma asked.

"Shorty Avis's place. One of them little outfits I was talking about. This one is here because Peg Cody lets it. Same as all the others on this side of the creek."

They rode toward the cabin, Kim calling, "Rocky."

A girl stepped out, a Winchester held on the ready. She asked, "Who you got there?"

Kim reined up and Yuma Bill slid down. Kim said, "I just met the stage. Yuma, meet Shamrock Avis, and don't be fooled by her size. Don't take much dynamite to blow a man to pieces."

Yuma lifted his hat. "Pleased to meet you, ma'am."

Frowning, the girl pinned dark eyes on the little man as if making a judgment of him. "Glad to know you, mister, but if you call me Shamrock, I'll blow up in your face."

Kim laughed. "You see, Yuma? Poison, that's what she is. Her mother named her Shamrock, but she's got other ideas, so folks call her Rocky."

"My mother, God rest her soul, made one big mistake in her life. That was naming me."

"Where's your pa?" Kim asked.

She gave him a questioning look, then said, "Out."

"Then you can feed a couple of strays. Yuma here has got a lunch, but he's saving it. Danged selfish, I claim."

"Sure, I'll rustle some grub," the girl said, "only I'll have a tough time explaining to Pa where it went to."

Rocky turned into the cabin. Yuma Bill asked softly, "What's this about her dad?"

"He just don't cotton to having anybody around who works

11

for Clawhammer. Plumb proddy, Shorty is, but you can't blame him. If I was in his boots, I wouldn't want to be living on the fringe of Clawhammer range, neither." Kim motioned to the cabin. "Go on in and get acquainted. I'll put my horse up."

CHAPTER 2

≈≈≈≈≈≈≈≈≈≈≈≈≈≈≈≈≈≈≈≈≈≈≈≈

ROCKY AVIS

KIM loitered outside the log barn after he had fed and watered his horse. It was pleasantly warm now, but clouds were rolling up above the Dragon Peaks on the other side of the valley. By midafternoon a storm would strike with a flurry of lightning and booming of thunder and probably a sharp downpour. Then the sky would clear and the freshly washed earth would steam under a hot sun.

Kim had been over most of the West, but this, to his way of thinking, was the most perfect spot he had ever seen. He liked the pines, the tiny-leafed aspens that shivered with each breath of wind, the columbines and mariposa lilies that were blooming now; he liked the wild smell of the high country that seemed to satisfy some inner hunger he had never fully analyzed. And he liked Rocky Avis who was as unspoiled and natural as this country in which she lived.

He moved toward the cabin, thinking of Shorty Avis who, by the grace of Clawhammer, took a precarious living from the wilderness. A little money invested in good stock could make this a profitable spread, but Shorty Avis had no money. If he or his neighbors did spread out, Peg Cody would, for her own protection, start making it rough for them. There was a chance she would anyhow when she quit feuding with Hank Dunning. Clawhammer could use the mesa for summer range.

Rocky was breaking eggs into a frying pan when Kim came into the cabin. Yuma Bill, his shoe box on his lap, was saying, "I just can't figure this business out. Brit Bonham was never one to make trouble for anybody, and it ain't right for him to be having trouble now."

Kim stopped in the doorway, a bony shoulder pressed against the jamb, and took off his hat. He was a tall man with a lean face that was weathered to the color of dark leather. Now he brushed back a stubborn lock of straw-colored hair that fell across his forehead, his blue eyes pinned on the girl's straight back.

An old thought came into his mind now, that Rocky Avis fitted the life she lived. It was rough, even the furniture in the cabin was homemade. Luxuries familiar to Peg Cody in her sprawling ranch house were unknown to Rocky. But somehow Kim had the notion that Rocky would take everything just the way it was if the choice was hers to make.

Rocky slid the frying pan to the front of the stove, stuffed the firebox full of aspen chunks, and turning saw Kim. She frowned as she set plates on the table, and then straightened to face him, slim hips pressed against the edge of the table.

"When it comes to trouble," she said, "you can get all the answers from Kim. Trouble is his business."

Yuma Bill glanced at Kim's face and lowered his gaze to the black-butted .44 holstered low on his thigh. He said, "I figured it was, but I still can't add it all up and get a sensible answer. It's Brit who's having the trouble, ain't it?"

"It adds up," the girl said evenly. "Brit Bonham's having trouble, all right, and so are a lot of other folks. With Kim it's a proposition of having too good a nose. He can smell trouble as far as a hound dog can smell coon."

"It's Brit Bonham I want to know about," the little man said. "What's that got to do with Logan?"

"Everything. It's all tied up into one package. A year ago Kim rode into Clawhammer and told Peg Cody he'd heard she needed a snake stomper. For a hundred dollars a month he'd stomp her snakes for her, and she's been paying him that ever since."

Kim hung his hat on a peg in the wall and dropped into a rawhide bottom chair. "When you get done gabbing about me, you'd better take a look at them eggs, Shamrock. I sure do hate burned eggs."

"You call me Shamrock again," the girl cried furiously, "and you'll get your eggs down the back of your neck."

Kim laughed softly as she turned to the stove. "I told you how it was, Yuma. There ain't even a mountain lion in these parts that'll stand up and look her in the eye."

Rocky, still facing the stove, said in the same angry voice, "Look at him, wearing fancy Justins and a Stetson that set him back fifty dollars. Silver spurs. He's even got gold in his teeth. Nobody else can afford stuff like that but Kim Logan."

"What are you getting so heated up for?" Kim asked. "I ain't robbed a bank."

"You're working for Peg Cody. Same thing." Rocky spooned the eggs into a platter that held a dozen pieces of salt side. She slammed the platter down on the table with a bang. "You wouldn't know how it is, trying to make a living

13

when any minute Peg Cody may take it into her head to run all of us off the mesa and take our places over."

"You're just dreaming things," Kim said mildly. "Peg's never bothered you."

"I'm not dreaming, I'm nightmaring." She pulled a pan of biscuits out of the oven, placed the biscuits on a plate, and set them on the table. "It isn't just Peg that makes me so mad. I know what to expect from a greedy woman. It's you I can't figure out. You've been doing what you call snake stomping all your life. What's it got you besides fancy duds? Nothing."

"I get along," Kim said, his voice still mild.

"Sure, you get along. You could drift out of here tomorrow and put everything you own in your pockets. You haven't got a dollar in the bank. You don't own a cow. Not even a calf. You could come here and work for thirty a month and beans, but no, that would mean chasing cows through the scrub oak, and you're no brush popper. You're . . . you're just a snake stomper."

She flounced to the stove, picked up the coffeepot and filled their cups, and flounced back to the stove again. "Come on and eat." She dropped into a chair, shoulders sagging as if suddenly tired. "I guess that anywhere we went, there'd be greedy people like Peg Cody and Hank Dunning. It's just that you seem different, Kim."

"Reckon I never thought about it," Kim said.

There was no more talk for a time. Kim and Yuma Bill ate, Kim wondering what had got into the girl. He had never seen her so angry, and apparently over nothing at all. When he was finished, he canted his chair back and rolled a smoke, eyes turning to Rocky's white face. He asked, "What set you off?"

"Nothing much." She got up and filled their coffee cups. "I just got to thinking about Brit Bonham who used his bank to help folks. Little folks like us along with the big ones like Peg Cody. Now look at the jam he got himself into."

The shoe box had been laying beside Yuma Bill's plate. He picked it up and scooted his chair back. He said, "I'm getting tired of being in the dark. What kind of a jam is Brit in?"

"Dunning aims to . . ." Rocky began.

"I'll tell it," Kim cut in. "He loaned too much money. That's all. Peg borrowed thirty thousand to stock her range. Clawhammer was in debt and pretty well run down when her old man died. Leastwise, that's what I hear. So when she borrowed from Brit, she went whole hog. It's too much, cattle prices being what they are. Looks like she and Brit are going broke together."

"She could save a hundred dollars a month by firing you," Rocky said sharply.

Kim shook his head. "I ain't flattering myself too much, I reckon, when I say she needs me and she knows it. Dunning would start pushing tomorrow if I wasn't around."

"Start pushing," the girl cried. "What do you think he's doing now?"

Kim grinned and winked at her. "He's just warming up to the job."

"You mean you've got Dunning bluffed?" Yuma Bill asked.

"Sort of. You see, he's a scheming sonuvagun who likes a sure thing. Fighting a woman is his size. Long as I'm working for Clawhammer, he ain't got a sure thing."

"He has if Peg doesn't fire Dutch Heinz," Rocky said. "I'd bet my bottom dollar he's sold out to Dunning."

Kim rose. "Let's ride, Yuma."

"You'd sure as hell better." It was Shorty Avis standing in the doorway, a cocked Winchester in his hands. "I told you before you wasn't wanted here. Now git afore I put a round window in your skull."

"Take it easy," Kim said. "You've got no quarrel with me."

"I've got a quarrel with Clawhammer," Avis bellowed. "Git, I said."

He was a tough bantam of a man, this Shorty Avis, with a knobby face and black piercing eyes that were alive with fury. Although Avis had never been friendly, Kim had liked him from the first because he instinctively liked any man who had a hard core of courage. Shorty Avis had it, or he wouldn't be here on the mesa telling Clawhammer men to stay off his land.

"Tell him, Dad," Rocky said quietly. "I was going to, but I hadn't got around to it."

Kim swung to face the girl. "Tell me what?"

"I'll tell you all right," Shorty barked. "You damned betcha I will. Dutch Heinz was up here early this morning. Said we had to get out of the country. Offered me a hundred dollars for this quarter section. Well, I ain't stirring my stumps, Logan. You go tell that woman you work for."

Kim studied Avis a moment, finding this hard to believe. Chores like that fell to him, and Peg had never indicated she wanted to oust the little fry.

"I'll talk to Peg," Kim said finally. "It don't smell right."

"Nothing smells right about Clawhammer." Avis gave him a wicked grin. "But I ain't gonna worry about you. I knowed all the time that Dunning would get you. He will afore sundown. I'm betting on it."

Kim moved toward Avis, warned by the triumph he sensed in the man. He said, "Keep talking, Shorty."

15

"I'll enjoy talking, and I'll enjoy seeing the finish. I sure as hell won't lose no tears when they plant you."

Kim put on his hat. "You know something, Shorty."

"You bet I know something." Avis backed out of the doorway. "Won't be long till you find out all about it. Now dust."

"What do you know, Dad?" Rocky crossed the room to stand beside Kim, and when her father's lips tightened into a stubborn line, she said with some sharpness, "Kim is taking a friend of Brit Bonham's into Ganado. In case you've forgotten, Brit is the best friend we have on this range."

"Now wait a minute," Kim said. "Have I done anything to make you think I wasn't your friend?"

"You're taking Peg Cody's orders," Rocky said.

He looked down at the girl's defiant face. "That don't mean I ain't a friend of yours."

"You won't be anybody's friend very long," Avis said. "Dunning sent Phil Martin over here with five HD hands. They're hunting for you now."

It took Kim a moment to fully grasp the significance of Shorty Avis's news. There had been a good deal of sparring between Clawhammer and HD in the year Kim had been in the valley, but not once had a Clawhammer man crossed the creek on HD range, nor had HD riders crossed to the Clawhammer side. Now if Martin, Dunning's ramrod, had come hunting for Kim, it must mean that Dunning had decided it was time to wind things up.

"Where are they?" Kim asked.

"Indian Springs the last I saw of 'em."

Kim stepped out of the cabin. "Let me have a horse, Shorty. We can't dodge 'em riding double."

"Thought you had a horse for me," Yuma said angrily.

"I have. At Clawhammer."

"You mean you figured on me riding double all the way to your damned ranch?" Yuma Bill shouted.

Kim swung to face him. "I didn't figure you'd be on that stage. Didn't make sense to me that a stranger would come toting a bunch of dinero into this country just to help out an old coot like Brit Bonham."

"Let him take Blackie, Pa," Rocky said.

Shorty Avis began to swell up. "When I let a Clawhammer man take a horse of mine, I'll be fit for the asylum . . ."

"You're fit for it if you don't," Rocky cut in. "It's Brit Bonham's friend who needs the horse. Anyhow, if we're able to stay here, it will be because Kim helps us."

"Helps us," Avis howled. "Why, this gun-toting varmint wouldn't help his own grandmother if that Cody woman told him to steal the gold teeth out of her head."

16

Kim started toward the barn, calling over his shoulder, "Fetch your sandwiches and come on, Yuma."

"You touch my horse and I'll . . ." Avis bawled.

"You'll do nothing," Rocky cried.

Kim went on, not looking back, and presently Yuma Bill caught up with him. He said, "I hope that girl runs the roost."

"She does," Kim said.

He threw gear on Shorty Avis's black gelding, tightened the cinches on the buckskin, and swung up. He said, "Let's ride."

Yuma Bill mounted, the shoe box gripped under one arm. They left the clearing on the run, Kim lifting a hand to Rocky. He had one glance at Shorty Avis, whose knobby face was filled with a dark and forbidding anger. Kim grinned, knowing Avis would do nothing more than rail at his daughter, for when the chips were down, it was Rocky who called the turn. Then Kim and Yuma Bill were in the aspens, the trail dropping swiftly toward the valley below.

CHAPTER 3

FOXES AND HOUNDS

THE trail curled downward in a series of looping switchbacks. Kim kept a fast pace, Yuma Bill following closely. An hour after leaving the Avis place, they reached a stand of pines, and here the trail straightened and ran directly down the slope. It was an old Ute trail that the Avises and their closest neighbors, the Fawcetts, used regularly on their trips to town. Kim had been over it many times. Now he pulled up, motioning for Yuma Bill to do the same. For several minutes he sat listening, the little man's eyes pinned on him.

Indian Springs lay to the right. Probably Phil Martin had stopped Shorty Avis there and asked about Kim. If Avis had known where he was, he would have told the HD man, for Avis wasn't smart enough to see that if Hank Dunning smashed Clawhammer, he would move across the creek and take the entire valley. Then Avis and the rest of the small fry would be worse off than they were now. Peg Cody was greedy as Rocky Avis had said, but she lacked the driving ruthlessness which was so much a part of Hank Dunning.

"How far to Clawhammer?" Yuma Bill asked.

" 'Bout three hours from here," Kim said, "if we went straight, but I don't figure we can. Chances are Martin and his bunch is off there somewhere." He motioned toward the southwest. "I'll feel a hell of a lot better if I know exactly where they are."

"You reckon they're after me?"

Kim shook his head. "Me. Dunning will figure his boys got you, so that ain't worrying him, but I've been in his hair ever since I got here. If they can make wolf meat out of me here in the hills, it'll be safer and maybe easier than doing the job in town."

"How would they know where to look?"

"I ride through these hills all the time. Part of my job is seeing that HD men stay on their side of the creek. Phil Martin knows that, so it's just a case of looking until they find me."

"Suppose they get you?"

Kim shrugged. "Then they'll move in. Our hands are with the cattle in the high country. Just Peg and an old man at the ranch. Chances are Dunning will burn the buildings, figuring Peg will sell for any offer he makes."

"Why hell, she wouldn't quit that easy, would she?"

"I ain't sure," Kim said thoughtfully. "She talks pretty tough, but she's never been through a range war. Her old man used to be the big push in the valley, but now the shoe's on the other foot."

"Hasn't she got a crew and a ramrod?"

"She's got a crew, but they ain't a very salty outfit. And Dutch Heinz, he's the ramrod, claims he ain't a fighting man."

He let it go at that. There was no point in telling Yuma Bill his suspicions. He had never been sure of Dutch Heinz and he was less sure now. He found it hard to believe that Peg had sent Heinz to warn Shorty Avis out of the country. On the other hand, it might be Dunning's idea to force the small ranchers into a war against Clawhammer. It would be like Dunning to get someone else to do his fighting for him.

"I don't savvy," Yuma Bill said. "Looks like this valley's big enough for both of 'em."

"Not for them it ain't," Kim said. "Let's ride."

He pulled off the trail and took a parallel course to it for a time. Phil Martin was a methodical sort of man who would systematically comb the hills, spreading his hands out so that they could cover the most ground. If Avis had not warned him, Kim would have ridden squarely into the HD guns. But now there was a chance he could slip through them.

The ground levelled off and Kim reined up again. He hipped around in the saddle. "Smell anything?"

Yuma nodded. "Dust. They've been through here."

"And they ain't far away." Kim motioned to his left. "Ganado Creek is yonder on the other side of this ridge. The can-

18

yon's deeper'n hell. We don't want to get run into it. Come on."

They circled a barrier of rocks and came again into the thick timber, the slope now quite gentle. Ten minutes later they broke out of the pines into a small park. An HD man was riding directly toward them, a burly cowhand named Tonto Miles.

For an instant all three were too stunned by surprise to do anything. Then Miles let out a squall, pulled his gun and fired, the bullet going high and wide. He cracked steel to his horse as Kim threw a slug at him and missed. Then he disappeared into the timber toward the trail.

"They're all around us," Kim said in disgust. "Ran smack into 'em."

Now other shouts sounded from the left. There was the thunder of hoofs swinging in from the trail as Kim put his horse into a run and headed directly across the clearing. Just before he reached the wall of timber, he looked back. Yuma Bill was ten feet behind him. Four men had reached the far side of the park, Phil Martin in the lead.

Whatever thought Kim had of stopping and making a fight of it left him. He had no idea how Yuma Bill would pan out in a showdown. Even if he was a good man, the odds were still too long.

Kim slanted down grade, hoping to get out of the rough country. If they could reach the flat, there was a chance they could outrun Martin's bunch, but the valley was still a long ways off. Besides, there was no telling how many others there were, or where they were. Shorty Avis had said six, but he might not have seen all of them, and Hank Dunning was not a man to do a half job.

Almost immediately Kim was forced to reverse direction, for two riders came into view directly in front of him. He angled back toward the rim, shaking his head at Yuma Bill's yell, "Thought we wanted to go the other way?"

"Come on," Kim called.

He knew now there was no way to avoid a fight, but if there was to be one, it would be on the battleground he picked. Here the pines were small and scattering. Martin and the three riders with him remained in sight, the distance between them unchanged. The other two had altered their course to parallel Kim's and Yuma Bill's, apparently aiming to block their escape to open country.

A mesa hill loomed ahead, and Yuma Bill bawled, "Damn it, you're letting 'em run us into a bottleneck."

Kim didn't answer. A gun cracked behind them, but the distance was too great and the bullet fell short. They reached the mesa hill and slanted up it, their horses laboring under them, red dust kicked up into a motionless cloud. Another gun roared. This time the bullet came too close for comfort. The climb had slowed Kim and Yuma Bill, and Martin had cut the distance between them.

They topped the crest and Kim waved for Yuma Bill to go on. He reined up, drawing gun. Martin, well ahead of the others, had reached the base of the hill. He looked up, close enough for Kim to see his broad face clearly, the sweeping sand-colored mustache, the crooked nose, even the smudge of red dust across his right cheek.

Martin gave out a frantic yell when he saw Kim's gun sweep down. He jerked his horse to a stop and plunged out of his saddle just as Kim fired. He dived toward a boulder as Kim squeezed off a second shot. Then he was under cover, bellied flat against the ground, and Kim was not sure whether he had scored a hit either time.

The three men following Martin had pulled and were firing, but it was too far for accurate shooting with hand guns. Kim wheeled toward his horse and snaked his Winchester from the boot, thinking that this might be as good a place as any to make a stand. He could keep Martin nailed behind the boulder until dark.

For the moment Kim had forgotten the other two riders who had bobbed up in front of them. Yuma Bill had swung back, yelling, "Come on, you idiot. They'll pot us like two ducks in a puddle."

Then Kim remembered. He looked for the two men, but they had disappeared. A slab of rock ran like an unbroken red wall from the base of the hill to the crest. They must have reined in behind it and were climbing to the top. Probably they wouldn't go that far. They'd dismount and hole up behind the rock slab. Then it would be like Yuma Bill said. The HD men would be forted up while Kim and Yuma Bill were in the open.

Kim whirled back to his horse and shoved the Winchester into the boot. He shouted, "Damn it, I told you to hightail."

"I never went off and left a man in a tight in my life," Yuma Bill shot back. "What the hell do you think I am?"

Kim swung into leather, motioning toward the red rim that inclosed the east side of the valley. "Dust," he called. "We'll make 'em come after us."

The cliff rose sheer above the mesa, a nest of boulders at its base. Kim pointed his horse toward the rocks. Yuma Bill swung in beside him, his angry voice rising above the clatter of hoofs, "You aiming to fly to the top?"

"Save your wind. We'll fort up."

They rode hard, hoofs beating against the rocky ground. When they were out of gun range, Kim pulled his buckskin down and looked back. No one was in sight. They went on, slower now, Yuma Bill eyeing him with sour disapproval. Minutes later they reached the boulders and swung in behind them. There was protection of a sort here, for the cliff formed an overhang so that the horses could be safely left at the base without danger of being seen from the rim.

Stepping down, Kim pulled his Winchester from the boot. "Take the horses back there." He motioned to the cliff. "Keep 'em there."

"Wait a minute, you danged chuckle-headed . . . ," Yuma Bill began.

But Kim didn't wait. He climbed to the top of the largest boulder and dropped flat on its smooth, weather-worn surface, eyes scanning the rocky flat in front of him. Still no one was in sight.

The ridge was about a mile long with a steep drop-off on every side except the east end which butted against the cliff; its surface was covered by small clumps of sagebrush, the smooth gray sweep of the flat broken only occasionally by a wind-gnarled cedar.

Westward beyond the break-off there was another steep slope dropping to the level floor of the valley. Kim could see the valley from this elevation, bright green where the sunlight was upon it, or freckled by islands of shadow. Clouds were boiling up now in a dark forbidding mass from the sullen Dragon Peaks. It would not be more than an hour until the clouds would cover the sky, and the sunlight would be blotted out for a time.

Ganado canyon lay just to the south, an ugly slash that ran from the great peaks of the continental divide to the valley. There its walls disappeared, and the creek which tumbled with white-laced violence from the high altitude slowed its course to make a series of looping meanders across the grass-covered valley.

Kim glanced up at the sky. The storm was moving in. Lightning had begun to flash in weird shifting veins above the Dragons, and thunder was rolling out its deep booming sounds, muted somewhat by distance. Kim brought his gaze back to the sage-carpeted flat. In one way this was a good position. Martin would find a direct attack difficult and costly, for the flat offered no shelter that was adequate for either man or horse.

On the other hand, the surface of this boulder where Kim lay might be a place of death. There was a break in the cliff to Kim's right. If an HD man climbed to the rim, he could look directly down upon the boulder. But right or wrong, Kim had picked his spot, and here the battle would be fought out to a decision.

21

CHAPTER 4

UNDER THE RIM

THE minutes dragged while the sky darkened and the ominous roll of thunder came closer. Then Kim heard the grating sound of boots on the side of the boulder. Turning, he saw that Yuma Bill was climbing toward him.

"Damn it," Kim said in exasperation. "I told you to stay with the horses."

Yuma Bill dropped down beside Kim. "They'll stay where I left 'em. Now maybe you'd like to tell me why you holed up here."

"Where would you be wanting to go?" Kim flung a hand out toward the flat in front of them. "Out there maybe?"

"We could have kept riding. If they had poked their heads up over the hill, we'd have blowed 'em off their necks."

"About the time we got far enough out there for them two hombres to notch their sights on us, we'd have got our heads blowed off. This was the only place we could go and keep out of their sight unless you wanted to go down into Ganado Canyon which I didn't."

Yuma Bill scowled, gaze swinging toward the lip of the canyon. "Reckon I forgot about that hole in the ground. I figgered on slanting back that way."

Kim jabbed a finger in the direction of the valley. "Clawhammer's off there. Just below where the creek comes out of the canyon. I figured we'd hole up here till dark and then make a run for it."

"How about the rim?" Yuma Bill jerked a thumb at the sullen red cliff behind them.

"That's the joker," Kim admitted. "If Martin's got a mountain goat in his outfit, he'll climb up there and we'll be caught like your two ducks in a puddle."

Yuma Bill rolled a smoke and fired it, his forehead furrowed. He said, "Logan, you've got all the time in the world, but I haven't. All that means anything to you is the hundred dollars a month you're getting; but I'm in this tight because I want to help a friend who gave me a hand once. Now I'm going to Ganado, and I don't aim to sit here till dark."

"Maybe we ain't so different at that," Kim said. "We both want to save our own hides, and you sure won't do Bonham no good if Martin plugs you and nabs your lunch box."

22

"You know what's in that box as well as I do," Yuma said sourly. "Brit's letter sounded like he didn't have much time, and here we are, nailed down on top of a damned rock."

"You still want to stay alive, don't you?" Kim demanded.

Yuma Bill glanced at the cliff behind him. "I ain't sure I'm going to."

"Git back with the horses," Kim said irritably. "What do you think I told you to say there for?"

"Maybe you need some help to stay alive. It's like you said this morning. I'd never get to that damned town if I struck out alone."

Kim's eyes had been searching the flat. He sat up, Winchester across his lap. "Take a look, friend. Five of 'em."

The HD riders had come into view where the rock slab levelled out on the flat. They reined up, remaining motionless for a time as they studied the cliff. Kim could not tell whether he and Yuma Bill had been seen or not, but in either case it seemed unlikely that Martin would close in.

"Five," Yuma Bill muttered. "Where's the other one?"

"Chances are he's crawling to the top," Kim answered. "It'll take him an hour or so. By that time we'll be under the overhang."

"Then we can't watch the other five and they'll walk in on us," Yuma said sourly. "I don't like it, Logan."

"I ain't in love with this deal either. What do you want to do, make a run for it?"

Yuma shook his head. "Not with them kind of odds."

They sat in silence, watching Martin and his men who had come on and then stopped just short of decent rifle range. Kim considered taking a few shots to worry them, and decided against it. The only shells he had for the Winchester were those in the magazine, and he'd need those and more before dark.

Kim gave some thought to climbing to the rim so Yuma Bill's back would be protected, and gave it up. The only break in the cliff for a mile or more to either side was a long trough-like slot that furnished precarious footing at best. If the other HD man had already started up, and Kim was sure he had, a climber below him would make a clear target.

There was nothing to do but wait, and Kim was not a man who found waiting easy. Nor did Yuma Bill seem to like it any better. He kept shifting from one part of the boulder to the other, smoking incessantly, eyes on the HD men who had dismounted and were hunkered in a tight little knot in front of their horses.

"Damn it," Yuma burst out. "Damn it to hell. I'm gonna ride out there and talk to 'em. You said it was you they wanted."

"Go ahead," Kim said. "You'll get halfway there if you're lucky and their shooting ain't good."

The little man beat a hand against the rock. "You haven't told me all of this."

"No," Kim admitted, "but I'll tell you now. Brit Bonham's spread himself so far that folks got to talking. It's my guess Dunning got the talk going, aiming to start a rush on the bank. Bonham ain't got the cash to pay off his depositors, so he'll have to close. He'll call in his loans. That breaks Peg Cody."

"So that's why you were so damned interested in keeping me alive?"

Kim nodded. "Only I don't figure it'll go quite like that. Dunning is a big depositor. If he pulls his money out, Bonham's finished. So somewhere along the line Dunning will make Bonham an offer for Peg's notes, and Bonham will have to sell 'em."

Yuma Bill tapped finger tips against the rock. "If I get my cash to Brit in time, I'll save the bank and while I'm doing that, I save Clawhammer."

"That's the size of it," Kim said. "Bonham told Peg when he was expecting you. Like a damned fool, he told Dunning, too. That's why we figured you'd never get to Ganado alive if I didn't stop the stage, so I stopped it just on the off chance you'd be on it."

"I still don't savvy why you're taking me to hellangone to get me to town," Yuma said sulkily.

"Reckon Peg wants to thank you." Kim grinned. "She's got a right nice way of thanking men who are on her side, but she's hell on the others."

It began to rain, a driving downpour with lightning breaking across the sky in vivid leaping flashes. "Come on," Kim shouted above the rolling thunder. "We've got to keep that lunch box dry, or your sandwiches will sure get damp."

Kim slid off the rock and dived under the overhang, Yuma Bill following. It was dry here, for there was little wind, and the rain was coming straight down in heavy slapping drops.

"Won't last long." Kim leaned his Winchester against the sandstone cliff, and untied his slicker from behind the saddle. "Stay here. This might be what they've been waiting for."

He stepped back into the rain, this time circling the big boulder instead of climbing to the top. He hunkered in front of it, his back hard against its wet surface so that a man on the rim above would have to lean out from the edge to see him.

The rain had spread a silver curtain across the flat, pelting it with fierce violence and hiding the five HD men who were out there. The summer storms seldom lasted more than a few minutes, but it might be long enough to give Martin the cover he needed.

A Winchester cracked from the rim, the bullet striking the rock and screaming off into space. Kim pressed back against the boulder, the beat of hoofs sweeping in from the sage flat coming clearly to him between the rolls of thunder. They had timed it perfectly, he thought. He was caught between the men riding in and the one on the rim.

He glimpsed them, shrouded by rain. He must have eased forward as he brought the Winchester to his shoulder, for the man on the rim squeezed off another shot, the slug slicing across the edge of the boulder, sending rock splinters flying. Martin and his riders were close enough now, and Kim began firing.

It was poor shooting, for the light was thin and the HD men were low in their saddles and riding fast. Kim missed with his first bullet, tagged Martin with his second, and missed with a third. He wiped his face as a slug from the rim slapped into the ground in front of him. A quick gust of wind swept the rain against him, blinding him for a moment. He squeezed his eyes shut and opened them, shaking his head and swearing.

Martin's men were angling a little now as they opened up with their Colts, bullets peppering the rock around Kim. He pronged back the hammer of his Winchester and squeezed off another shot, knocking an HD rider out of his saddle in a rolling fall.

A scream sounded shrilly through the heavy roar of guns, a human scream of wild, absolute terror. A body thudded into the rocks to Kim's left, but he had no time to see who it was. He was working his Winchester steadily; he heard Yuma Bill cut loose with his Colt. A moment later he saw that the fight had been won. Martin had stopped to help the fallen man up behind him, right arm swinging in a wide signal for retreat.

Yuma Bill was beside Kim saying, "That yahoo on the rim fell off. Sure got busted up."

Another Winchester was cracking from the rim, but the bullets were not slanting down at Kim and Yuma Bill. They were being aimed at the HD riders who were in full retreat across the flat. Kim emptied his rifle at them, puzzled by what had happened. He did not know how much damage he had inflicted on Martin's crew, but it must have been considerable to have knocked the fight out of them as effectively as he had.

Kim rose, glancing at Yuma Bill who was staring after the retreating HD crew. The little man brought his eyes to Kim and wiped the rain from his face, blinking and shaking his head. He asked, "Who's up there?"

"I don't know, but I've got a hunch."

Wheeling, Kim glanced at the broken body of the man who had fallen. He had seen the fellow a few times in Ganado with Phil Martin, but he didn't know his name. Just a gun-handy drifter who had taken Dunning's wages and made a bad bargain. As Kim ran past him to his horse, a thought cut its way through his mind, It could be me lying *there*.

He slipped his Winchester into the boot, and stepping into saddle, brought his buckskin around. He rode out of the shelter of the overhang into the rain. It had slacked off now to a fine mist; the lightning was gone from the sky. The storm had moved on, but the smell of rain was heavy in the air and the red sandstone cliff was wet and bright.

Yuma Bill shouted, "What are you up to?"

"Finding something out," Kim said.

He rode directly away from the cliff until he could see the rim. Rocky Avis was standing there, a slim boyish figure in a man's shirt and trousers, a rifle in her hand. She waved when she saw Kim, calling, "Both of you all right?"

"Nary a scratch," he answered, reining his horse around. "How'd you come to buy into this ruckus?"

"I figured it was a good idea to keep you two alive," she said. "I got up on the rim after you left and watched them give you a run. Then when you forted up down there, I thought you might need a hand, so I rode over. What about that hairpin who went over the edge?"

"Dead."

She shook her head. "I'm sorry."

"What for? He wouldn't have been sorry if he'd plugged me or Yuma Bill in the back."

"I know, but it seems a poor thing to die for. He was leaning over trying to get a bead on you when I saw him. I got up close before he knew I was there. I told him to hook the moon. He jumped and took a step back and over he went."

"Well, you sure did a job for us. It would have been a little rough if they'd kept coming in." He cuffed back his hat. "Rocky, this ain't good. You're into the fight now if they saw who you were."

"We're in the fight anyway. Pa's just too stubborn to see it. You two better get along now."

"We'll have to take the body in."

"Tie him on his horse. I'll have Pa take him to town. You'd better make tracks while you can. They might still give you trouble."

Kim shook his head. "They had a stummickful, but we'll find his horse and leave him here. You hightail home, and get it through Shorty's bonehead that Dunning's the man he'd better be scared of."

26

"I'll tell him, but he won't believe it. Not after seeing Dutch Heinz this morning."

She waved and disappeared over the lip of the rim. Kim rode back to Yuma Bill. He said, "It was Rocky Avis. She don't see this business like Shorty does. She trailed us, figuring we might need a hand."

"So a woman saves our lives," the little man said. "I don't like that, Logan."

"I do. It was kind o' touchy there for a minute."

"Most women don't forget what you owe 'em," Yuma said bitterly. "I know."

"Rocky's different," Kim said, and rode past Yuma Bill to the break in the cliff.

The dead man's horse had been tied there to a small cedar. Kim led him back to the rocks, saying nothing as they lashed the body across the saddle. Later, riding across the flat steaming now under a hot sun, he glanced at Yuma Bill, wondering what was in the man's mind.

Suddenly Yuma felt Kim's eyes and turned his head. He burst out, "I hope to hell you know what you're doing. If we're too late to save Brit's bank, I'll take it out of your hide."

"I'm in this to earn my hundred dollars a month, you know," Kim said. "Remember?"

"That's got nothing to do with . . ."

"I just got to thinking about what you said. Then I got to asking myself how you got so damned high and mighty that you could preach to me."

Yuma Bill's craggy face softened. "So that's it. Well, I didn't aim to preach. Just seemed like you had things twisted a mite."

"Like what?"

"Like putting your orders above saving Brit Bonham's bank."

"Hell, I'm just doing my job. Strikes me that when a man takes a job, he'd better do it."

"That ain't enough. I'm more'n twice your age, Logan. That's given me twice as much time to think as you've had. Now I ain't saying I ain't done my share of ornery things, but somewhere along the line I've found what pays a man and what don't."

"My job pays me," Kim said, "and pretty damned good."

"No, you're getting short-changed unless you're in love with this Peg Cody. It's like this, Logan. Every man sows some seed, it grows, and it's gonna be harvested whether he does it or someone else does. Now what kind of seed have you sowed?"

"Aw, get a pulpit," Kim said resentfully.

Yuma Bill smiled. "Well, maybe I oughtta, but you started

27

this sermon, and I aim to finish it. It's short and sweet. You get to the last hill. We all do, sooner or later, and I'm a hell of a lot closer to it than you are. You take a look back and you see all them crops you've planted. If you've used the right seed, you go over the range feeling purty damned good about everything. But this other hombre, the one who didn't give a whoop what he planted, why, I reckon he's gonna burn in the hellfire the parsons talk about."

"I suppose you know all about women, too," Kim said. "You seem to know about everything else."

"I know a little all right," Yuma said, bitterness creeping into his voice. "I've always had a little money, and that draws women like honey draws bees." He scratched his nose. "But maybe I had your little Rocky girl all wrong. If she loves you, she won't be holding you in her debt. Some women ain't capable of love. Maybe she is."

"Love me? Why hell, she's just a kid . . ."

"Nineteen or twenty, ain't she? Old enough to be in love. I can't see no other reason for her getting so huffy with you at noon if she wasn't. Or risking her hide to save yours."

Kim let the talk die. It was something he had not thought about before, and he dismissed it as an old man's idle talk. But there was one thing he did know. The last person in the world he wanted to hurt was Rocky Avis.

CHAPTER 5

CLAWHAMMER

THE SUN tipped down behind the Dragon Peaks and dusk flowed across the valley, the purple twilight giving a sense of weird unreality to it. Darkness moved in, and to the west the Dragons became sharp black points against a pale sky. Then the last trace of light above the horizon died, and the mountains were lost to sight, their lines fading into indistinct blurs.

When Kim and Yuma Bill rode down off the last bench to the valley floor, the darkness was so complete that the distant lights of Ganado gleamed like clustered stars that had dropped from the black sky. They turned toward Clawhammer, following a bend in the bench, and presently the lamp-brightened windows of the big ranch house came into sight.

Ten minutes later they reined up under the ancient cottonwoods that had prompted Peg's father to build his house here. A man called from the corrals, "Who is it?"

A dog bounded toward Kim, barking in short angry yaps. Kim said, "All right, Nero," and when the dog was silent, he called, "It's me, Limpy."

Kim dismounted and waited. The man drifted up out of the darkness, asking, "Any trouble, son?"

"A little," Kim said. "Peg in the house?"

"Yeah, she's there. Just got back from town. Go on in. I'll take care of your horses."

"Come on, Yuma." Kim swung around and crossed the yard, a little soft now from the afternoon rain, and stepped up on the porch. "Scrape the mud off, Yuma. She's hell on a man who totes mud into her house."

"I respect a clean woman," Yuma Bill said, "if she don't make a religion out of it."

"She don't." Kim cleaned his boots on the scraper and went in. He called, "Peg." The smell of coffee and frying ham was a fragrance in the house that sharpened the hunger in Kim. He shouted "Peg" a second time, and crossed the living room to the kitchen door, Yuma Bill following, the shoe box under his arm.

Peg Cody turned from the big wood range where she was frying ham, and gave Kim a quick smile. She was tall, almost as tall as Kim and about the same age. Her hair seemed even redder than usual in the lamplight, and her hazel eyes that could reflect a smile or be bright with wild and sudden anger were warm now with pleasure at seeing Kim. She was a temperamental woman with a disposition that swung easily from one extreme to the other, and Kim had learned long ago to walk easy until he read the mood which possessed her at the moment.

"Come in, Kim," Peg said. "I had a hunch you'd be dragging in as hungry as an old bear in the spring, so I fixed a little extra. I just got back from town."

"This is Yuma Bill," Kim said. "Yuma, meet Miss Cody."

"I'm glad to know you," Peg said pleasantly. "I've been worried about both of you all day."

The little man stood with all the height he possessed, hat dangling from one hand, the shoe box under the other arm. He said, his voice cool, "Howdy, ma'am."

She turned back to the stove. "Brit Bonham calls you his friend. The way I see it, that's the finest thing one man can call another."

Yuma Bill nodded, her words thawing him. "Thank you, ma'am. I'm proud to be Brit's friend."

She motioned toward the back door. "Wash up, Kim. Supper's ready."

Kim crossed the kitchen to the back porch, pumped a pan of water, and stepped aside for Yuma Bill to wash. He moved to the end of the porch and looked out across the valley that seemed to stretch on and on into black eternity, and thought of the first time he had seen Peg a year ago. He had ridden in from Ganado on his buckskin, tired and gaunt and looking tough enough to impress the devil himself. He must have impressed Peg, for she had hired him at once with no more recommendation than the toughness of his appearance.

In the year since then he had kept on riding, but with a definite purpose. As soon as he had caught the full picture, he told Peg that there would never be peace in the valley until Hank Dunning was dead. On at least two occasions he had prodded Dunning until he thought the man would go for his gun, but the HD owner had wanted none of it.

Kim had puzzled over it many times. Dunning did not give the appearance of being a coward. Almost everyone in the valley was afraid of him, for he was fast with the bone-handled .45 he wore on his right thigh. Still, he had turned his back and walked off.

Yuma Bill emptied his pan over the railing and said, "Yours, Logan." He dried and drifted back into the kitchen. Kim washed and combed his hair, thinking that in the year he had worked for Clawhammer, he still did not really understand Peg. He had never felt the sting of her tongue, although he had seen her go into towering rages when some of her riders made a mistake or failed to carry out an order. She must have sensed from the first that he was one man who would take nothing from her, and she had treated him accordingly.

Kim did know one thing. Clawhammer meant everything to her. For that reason she had gambled recklessly in borrowing so much money from Bonham. But, perhaps failing to foresee that Bonham's bank might close her out, she had not considered it a gamble. She seldom discussed the ranch business with Kim, and she never asked his advice. Their relationship had been strictly that of employer and employee. Still, she had the power to stir him as she could stir any man who possessed a normal man's desires; she had often gone out of her way to be with him. Yet after a year on Clawhammer, Kim had a feeling that her deepest thoughts and ambitions were secrets known only to herself.

"Break your leg out there?" Peg called.

He went into the kitchen, patting the stubborn cowlick that never stayed in place. He said, "Yeah, broke my leg."

"Have to shoot you. No room on this spread for a useless horse." She motioned to a chair. "Sit down. I'm so hungry I'm going to start eating whether you two do or not."

It was a good meal of ham, beans, fried potatoes, biscuits,

apple butter, and hot black coffee. Kim had often eaten with her when the crew was gone, and he had never had a bad meal at her table. It was one of the many things he liked about her. She could ride a horse with the best; she made a hand when she was needed, but there was this other side to her. She kept the house immaculate, she made her own dresses, and she baked the best chocolate cake he had ever tasted.

"Better fetch your crew in," Kim said, reaching for the ham. "Dunning's fixing to force a fight."

"Then he'll get one."

"And we'd better be ready. I don't like the notion of your being here with just Limpy, and I won't be earning my wages if I sit here keeping the seat of my pants warm."

She frowned, throwing him a sharp glance as if not liking his advice. "I'm not afraid of Dunning, but I am worried about our cows. That's where my boys belong, and that's where they'll stay."

"We had some trouble," Kim said.

She rose and went to the stove for the coffeepot. "Let's hear about it."

Kim told her what had happened, leaving out only the fact that Rocky Avis had bought into the fight. He wished he had told Yuma Bill to hold his tongue about it. Glancing now at the little man, he was relieved to see that he had finished eating. Yuma Bill had canted his chair back against the wall and was busying himself with a cigarette, apparently satisfied to let Kim do the talking.

Peg drank her coffee and put the cup down. "I don't like it, Kim. I don't like it at all, but it doesn't change anything. I've contracted to deliver five hundred head of steers in Durango this fall. I've got to do that. Nothing else is important."

"Your life is," Kim said doggedly.

"My life isn't in danger. We have law here, Kim. You're overlooking that."

"Law?" Kim laughed shortly. "What kind of law does Ed Lane give this valley? He's picked his side, and it ain't ours."

She gave him a close questioning glance. "That's the way it's got to be, Kim. You're all the army I can afford to hire."

Kim rose, suddenly angry. He had no illusions about himself. He was a good man to a certain point, but no man, regardless of how good he was, could fight Hank Dunning's outfit. It was up to every Clawhammer hand from the ramrod, Dutch Heinz, on down to old Limpy.

"I ain't one to tell my boss how to run her business," Kim said sharply, "but I've been through some range wars and I know how they go. Likewise I know about sheriffs like our

31

great Ed Lane. When Dunning's ready to finish us off, Lane will go fishing."

"All right, Kim," she said, her tone matching his. "Don't tell me how to run my business. I hired you to use your gun. Use it."

"I will, damn it." Kim pounded the table with his fist. "I'll use my gun, but I don't cotton to being chased by Martin and five of his boys. Call your hands down and let me take 'em across the creek. I'll finish this in one night, and then you can raise your beef in peace."

Peg was on her feet then, face red with anger. "My boys are cow hands. You're the snake stomper. Now you can either stomp or drift. This is the first time you've smelled powder-smoke, and it looks like you don't care much for the smell."

Wheeling, Kim stalked toward the door. Yuma Bill said quietly, "You're losing a good man, Miss Cody. As good as you'll find."

"Wait, Kim," Peg cried, and ran after him. "I'm sorry. I shouldn't have said that."

Kim turned, glaring at her. "You're damned right you shouldn't have said it. Maybe you don't know it, but you're in a hell of a fight. The only way to win is to get the jump on Dunning and finish him."

"Let me think about it." She put a hand on his arm, a quick impulsive gesture. "It's just that I don't want to force trouble if I can help it. I . . . I guess the money I owe Bonham is making me crazy."

"What about Bonham?" Yuma Bill asked. "His bank all right?"

Peg nodded. "There's been no run yet, but you'd better be in town by nine in the morning."

"I aim to." Yuma Bill got to his feet and reached for the shoe box. "I couldn't figure out why Logan wanted to fetch me here first. I still can't, but if Brit's all right, it don't make no difference."

"He's tired, Kim," Peg said. "Take him out to the bunk-house. Then you come back."

She was suddenly contrite, and that was not like her. She seldom as far as Kim knew, apologized about anything or admitted a mistake, but in her way she was doing both now. A small inviting smile lay in the corners of her mouth; her eyes were half closed as if she were enjoying the anticipation of something which lay ahead.

Kim nodded and turned toward the living room door. He stopped, suddenly tense, hand dropping to gun butt. Someone had ridden up and was crossing the yard, spurs jingling. Kim backed away to the table, and waited there until the man came into the kitchen. It was Dutch Heinz.

32

Kim glanced briefly at Yuma Bill who had set the shoe box down on the table again. Heinz stood in the doorway, spread-legged. He nodded at Peg, gave Kim a cool stare, and brought his gray eyes to Yuma Bill. He was a stocky man with a wide flat nose, and possessed of an overbearing insolence which never failed to arouse resentment in Kim when he was around the man.

"Who's this?" Heinz asked, motioning to Yuma Bill.

"It's Bonham's friend that we were expecting," Peg said.

"Bonham's friend, eh? So Logan got him off the stage. Any trouble?"

"A little," Kim said.

Heinz walked toward the table. Yuma Bill threw a questioning glance at Kim and brought his eyes back to Heinz, furrowed face dark with trouble.

"Things don't look good in town, Dutch," Peg said. "There's talk of the bank being shaky."

Heinz said nothing. Kim did not guess what was in the man's mind until he reached the table. Without a word he picked up the shoe box, snapped the cord that was tied around it, and jerking the lid off, upset the box. Bundles of greenbacks fell on the table, more greenbacks than Kim had ever seen in his life before.

Yuma Bill cried out, a wild incoherent sound, and grabbed for his gun. Heinz, expecting that, wheeled and struck him, a brutal blow that sent the little man crashing against the wall. His feet slid out from under him and he sat down, glassy-eyed. Stooping, Heinz pulled Yuma Bill's gun and threw it on the table.

Kim was caught off-guard. It seemed senseless, so senseless that he was momentarily stunned by it. Then a wild rage was in him; he lunged at Heinz, left fist swinging to the man's wide jaw. Heinz went down, falling hard. Peg screamed, "No, stop it," but neither man heard. Heinz rolled, grabbed for his gun, but he was dazed and a little slow. Kim jumped at him, a heel coming down on Heinz's wrist and bringing a yell of pain out of him.

Peg screamed again, "Quit it, you fools."

Kim stepped back. Heinz lifted himself to his hands and feet, and looked up. There was a wildness in his gray eyes, and a driving hatred.

"You've got your gun," Kim said quietly. "Get up and make your play."

But Peg was between them then. "No more of this. You understand? Clawhammer has enough enemies without fighting among ourselves."

"His idea." Heinz got up, feeling of his injured wrist. "It's time we found out who's running this outfit."

"It's past time you found out," Peg cried furiously. "I'm running it, and I tell you I won't have this brawling."

"Then fire him," Heinz bellowed. "He's drawing good wages for nothing."

"I still need him," Peg said, her voice ominously low. "You've got a good job, Dutch. Do you want it or not?"

For a moment Heinz said nothing. He stood with his head dropped forward on his great shoulders, his breath sawing into the quiet. Then he said, "Yeah, I want to keep it, which same you know, but you don't seem to know you're making a hell of a mistake. Your dad wouldn't have made no such mistake."

Peg stepped forward, and for a moment Kim thought she was going to strike Heinz. She said, her voice controlled, "I'm not my dad. Why aren't you with the crew?"

Heinz ignored the question. He motioned toward the money. "Use your head, Peg. Look at that. All the dinero you need to pay off every debt you owe. What the hell difference does it make about Bonham and his bank. This is here for the taking."

Peg glanced at Kim, biting her lower lip and saying nothing. Yuma Bill was on his feet now, a hand raised to his face where Heinz had hit him. He said bitterly, "I suppose I was brought here so you could steal my money. That right, Logan?"

"No," Kim said.

But Heinz had eyes for no one but Peg. "Bonham couldn't trace it. Nobody could. Take it in first thing in the morning and pick up them notes. I'll fix it so nobody will ever see the old man again." He motioned toward Yuma Bill. "And if Logan thinks as much of Clawhammer as you allow, he won't squawk."

For a moment there was silence except for the metallic hammering of a clock on a corner shelf. Kim, too, was watching Peg. For that moment it seemed to him she was being tempted by what Heinz had said.

Then she said, "No. Get back to where you belong, Dutch."

Heinz took a long breath and shook his head as if this was beyond his comprehension. He moved to the door, then turned, cuffing his hat, and gave Kim a straight look. He said, "I'll kill you, Logan. That's a promise."

"Shorty Avis said you'd been up there telling him to get out of the country. That his idea, Peg?"

"Tell him, Peg," Heinz said. "Tell him, or I will."

"No, it wasn't my idea," Peg said quickly. "I won't ask you again, Dutch. Get back to the crew."

Heinz's meaty lips fell apart. "Why, you . . ." He stopped

34

as if reading something in Peg's face. Then he said heavily, "All right. Play it your way." Turning, he tramped across the living room and left the house.

Peg said nothing until the beat of hoofs came clearly to them. Then she nodded at Yuma Bill. "I'm sorry this happened, but there's no use apologizing for it now. You go get some sleep. I'll have breakfast for you before sunup. You'll get to town in time before the bank opens. And Kim, you come back in. I want to talk to you."

CHAPTER 6

A KISS

THERE was a light in the bunkhouse. The old chore man, Limpy, was pulling off his boots when Kim and Yuma Bill came in. He looked up, started to say something, and closed his mouth when he saw their bleak faces.

"Get your sleep," Kim said curtly. "We'll dust out of here afore sunup."

Yuma Bill, his nerves wound tight, said, "This is a hell of a thing you fetched me into, Logan."

"I know," Kim said, "I know," and left the bunkhouse.

When Kim returned to the house, he saw that Peg had moved the lamp from the kitchen to the big oak table in the living room. She was not in sight, but the door of her bedroom was ajar, and she called, "Sit down, Kim. I'll just be a minute."

He walked around the room, too restless to sit down. He stood for a moment in front of the picture of Sam Cody, Peg's father. It was covered by glass; its heavy gilt frame was ornately carved. Somehow the fancy frame with its curlicues did not seem to fit the heavy-featured, boldly arrogant face. Even his eyes were insolent. They glared at Kim from under bushy brows as if resenting Kim's presence in the house.

A pusher, Kim had been told in Ganado, a driver who slammed through to whatever he wanted, and to hell with anybody who was in his way. Dutch Heinz had worked for him, and he had, Kim thought, learned his methods from old Sam. But Peg didn't even look like him. She was different. She had to be. She was fighting for Clawhammer's life, but her ways were not the ways of her father.

Kim did not know Peg had come up behind him until she said, "You think I look like him?"

35

He turned, catching the rich smell of a French perfume Fred Galt had recently put on the shelf of his Mercantile in Ganado. She had changed from her riding skirt and blouse to a blue dress with a tight-fitting bodice, a dress designed to make a man instantly aware that she was a woman, roundly molded and appealing.

"No," Kim said. "You don't look like him at all."

"Why not?"

He held his answer a moment, letting her see the admiration that was in him. This was the side of her that he liked; he did not like the other side that made her wear straight-lined mannish clothes and ride on roundup when she could have hired another hand.

Kim turned, motioning to the picture. "He looks like a tough hand. Kind o' like a bull with his mind made up."

Peg laughed. "He was that way, all right. He drove a herd into the valley a long time ago. It was just after the mining boom was tapering off, and there were a few ranchers along the creek who didn't take to being pushed." She stopped, her eyes thoughtful. "But they got pushed just the same. He was a fighting man, Kim, and a good one."

"There's fighting men and then there's fighting men," he said. "I don't reckon your dad and me would have hitched."

"Why?"

"I don't like anybody who ain't willing to live and let live," he said bluntly. "The ten-cow outfits like Shorty Avis's have a right to make out without somebody pushing 'em out of the country."

She walked away from him and sat down on the leather couch, smoothing her dress over her knees. "I don't see it that way, Kim. If they aren't big enough and tough enough to hold what they've got, they won't last."

"They'll last if they're let alone."

She shook her head. "But they won't be let alone. The world I see all around me is made for big people, so I aim to be big, so big that all the valley will be mine. It's not just money that I want. It's respect if you want to call it that, or prestige, or whatever. I'll have it, Kim. You'll see."

"What about the Avises?"

"I don't really care one way or the other. Right now I don't need the mesa range. Maybe I will tomorrow. If I do, they'll go." She gave him a close look. "Why are you interested in them? Is it the girl?"

He shook his head. "I just cotton to folks who don't run easy."

"Sit down." She patted the leather seat. "I was wondering if I should be jealous."

"No reason for you to be jealous of anybody." He dropped

36

down beside her. "Looks like I'll be drawing my time in a day or two."

"Kim!" She laid a hand over his. "You wouldn't pull out when the ship's sinking, would you?"

"No place for me here. Not if Heinz stays."

"Don't get your neck bowed." She squeezed his hand. "I have some virtues along with my faults. Being loyal is one of them. Dutch was a kid wrangler when Dad came to the valley. He knows the cattle business, and I owe him a job if he wants it. If he doesn't, you're in line."

"Not me," he said quickly. "Not if it means pushing folks like the Avises."

"You aren't being very smart." She drew her hand back. "None of these little outfits are worth us quarreling over. Give them every chance and they'll never be anything but what they are."

"They've got the right to try," he said hotly. "Or just stay like they are if that's the way they want it."

She leaned back, one hand clasping a knee. "Kim, I need you. It's a funny thing how much you've done for me without actually doing anything. Hank Dunning is a lot like Dad was. He goes after what he wants. If you hadn't come, he'd have us backed against the wall by now."

"I've played my string out unless I do something," he said.

"I don't think so."

"I know so. It's smash or get smashed. Tomorrow we save the bank. Dunning won't like it a little bit. He'll move, and that's when you'll need every man you've got."

She closed her eyes. "Kim, listen to me. I'm ambitious. You know that, but you don't know how I've laid awake nights, dreaming about what I'm going to do and thinking about where Dad made his mistakes. A bad winter and low beef prices almost ruined Clawhammer. I suppose it was worry that killed him. Well, I'm not going to make his mistakes, but I'm a woman, so I'll use the weapons the Lord gave a woman."

"What are they?"

She laughed, and bringing her knees up under her chin, she faced him, her eyes bright. "Dutch is one weapon. You're another."

"I ain't so sure about me," he said roughly. "You've got use for me next week. Or next month. By that time Dunning will be dead or you'll be licked. Either way, you won't need me after that."

"I'll always need you, Kim."

She got up and walked across the room, her back to him, her skirt making a tight fit across her hips. She reached the tabie, and turning, raised her eyes to him. For a moment she stood there, smiling. She ruffled the pages of a mail order catalog that lay in front of her, then pushed it away.

"You believe that, don't you?" she asked in a voice that was close to pleading.

"No. You need somebody. It don't have to be me."

"It's got to be you," she said quietly, "but there are times when I don't understand you. I wake up in the night thinking about you, and then it seems you're almost a stranger."

"I get the same notion about you."

"Oh, you're talking crazy. I've lived in the valley since I was a little kid. I don't have any secrets, Kim."

"You do in your head," he told her.

She came back to the couch and sat down again beside him. "I've told you the only secret I have. It's why I mortgaged everything to Brit Bonham, hoping to put Clawhammer back to where it was before Dad lost so much. It's why I hired you. It's why I do everything I do." She leaned back, hands laced over her knees again, long legs swinging. "I'm going a long ways, Kim, but I have one fear. Maybe I'll be alone when I get there. Then it won't be any fun."

For some reason Kim thought of what Rocky Avis had said that noon about Peg's being a greedy woman, about his being a snake stomper without a dollar in his pocket. That wasn't true, but compared to Peg Cody, he might as well have been broke.

"I don't savvy," he said finally. "Not exactly, but I know one thing. A gunslinger ain't fit to go along to where you're headed."

"Depends on the gunslinger. Why do you think I hired you in the first place?"

"Dunno."

"It's very simple, Kim. You aren't like most of the grub line riders who come through here. I've always prided myself on my knowledge and judgment of men. I didn't make a mistake in you."

He looked at her curiously. "How am I different?"

"I guess it's just that there's more to you. I mean, well, like insisting on taking the crew across the creek to finish Dunning. Most men who had a good thing would follow my orders and be satisfied."

"I've got my notions about how to do a job," he said.

"I know," she said softly. "You have a good many notions, Kim, strong ones. I can't help wondering where you got them. Tell me about yourself. Who your folks were and where they came from and everything."

"Nothing to tell. I was born in Missouri. Folks moved out to New Mexico and my ma died of smallpox. My dad died a couple of years later. I threw in with a salty bunch when I was sixteen. Been riding ever since till I got here."

"What was your mother like?"

"I don't remember her very well," he said, and let it go at that. It was one thing he would not talk about.

"I don't remember much about my mother, either," she said. "She had red hair like mine, and I do remember the terrific quarrels they had, but you know, Kim, they were terribly in love with each other." She laughed, wrinkling her nose at him. "We'd quarrel, too, wouldn't we?"

She had drawn her legs up under her, and she was leaning toward him, her face quite close to his, red lips lightly pressed. He put his arm around her and drawing her to him, kissed her. In that instant she became a living flame in his arms, her hands reaching up to hold him, her lips passionate and clinging.

Later, when she drew away, her hands came up to his cheeks and caressed them with a touch. "Kim, Kim," she murmured, "you were so slow. I'm getting pretty old, you know. Twenty-three. Almost an old maid."

"You're talking crazy now," he said. "A little encouragement would bring any man in the valley walking to you on his knees. Even Hank Dunning, I reckon, if you wanted him."

She straightened, suddenly tense. "Kim, are you out of your mind?"

"Maybe. Kissing you would put any man out of his mind." He rose, looking down at her long slim body, her lips that were smiling again. "I can't ask you to marry me. Not yet."

"Why?" she demanded. "Don't tell me you never thought about it. After a year on Clawhammer . . ."

"I've thought about it all right." He paused, wondering what had happened to him today. This was what he had wanted; what any man would want, a pretty wife and a big spread. But now that the opportunity was here, he could not take it. "Just another one of my notions. Seems like I've got to bring something to you besides my hands and a gun."

She looked at him for a long moment, her face grave, then she shook her head. "Don't make a mistake now, Kim. Our life wouldn't be all sweetness and sunshine, but there would be other things to make up for it."

"Maybe I'm thinking about Dutch Heinz," he said. "Or maybe it's just that I don't want to be Mr. Peg Cody."

He left the house, leaving her staring after him, frowning as if she were deeply troubled. He walked slowly toward the bunkhouse, wondering how big a fool he had been. If he had asked her to marry him, she would have said yes. He was as sure of that as he had ever been sure of anything. But he had

39

not asked her, and the right moment might never come again.

Suddenly Kim was aware of the smell of a cigarette; he saw the bright tip of it glowing in the darkness. He reached for his gun and then drew back his hand at once, realizing that an enemy would not give his presence away so carelessly. He said, "Well!"

"Waiting," Yuma Bill said. "Just waiting. I ain't of a mind to trust anybody after what happened tonight."

"Damn it, you can trust me," Kim said angrily. "Are you making out you can't?"

"No, I ain't," the little man said. "I was kind o' dozing after Heinz cracked me, but I got the notion you sort of whittled him down to size."

"Well, why ain't you sleeping?"

"Why, it's just a matter of arithmetic. Anyway I count, you still add up to just one man, so I'll stay awake till this dinero is in Brit's safe."

"It'll be there by nine in the morning."

They walked on toward the bunkhouse. Then Yuma Bill said, "She's playing with you, boy."

Kim gripped the little man's arm. "You damned pussy-footing window peeper. I oughta . . ."

Yuma Bill jerked away, angry. "I ain't no window peeper. I just knew how she'd perform. You think you're gonna marry her, don't you? Sweet as the bottom of the sugar bowl, wasn't she?"

"Yeah, sweet enough," Kim said. "But I dunno about marrying her. Maybe I'll never have another chance."

"Then you'll be lucky. If you let her, she'll use you and drop you when she's done with you. I know because I've been through the mill."

"Women ain't all alike. Just because . . ."

"Her kind are. I can read her brand easy as I could the Clawhammer iron on a steer. She's thinking first, last, and always of Peg Cody, and she'll never change. You'll see."

"You're too damned suspicious," Kim muttered, and went into the bunkhouse.

But he did not sleep for a long time. He lay staring at the dark ceiling, more discontented with himself and his life than he had ever been before. In spite of himself, he mentally compared Rocky Avis, sarcastic and sharp-tongued and at times cruelly honest, with Peg, and it surprised him that Peg was not flattered by that comparison. Still, he understood her as he had never understood her before, and he could not doubt the truth of what she had told him about herself.

CHAPTER 7

THE HOUR OF NINE

THEY ate breakfast by lamplight, Peg silent and oddly aloof, her shoulders slack with weariness as if she had not slept during the night. Only now and then did her eyes brush Kim's face, and they told him nothing.

When they finished eating, Yuma Bill rose, the shoe box under his arm. He said, "Thank you, ma'am. I hope my coming will be of some help to you as well as Brit."

"You're saving Clawhammer," she said simply. "I'm the one who's doing the thanking."

Kim drank his coffee and got up. "Time to go. I oughtta be back a little after noon. Then I'll stay here unless you change your mind about hitting Dunning before he hits you."

"I'm not changing my mind, Kim," she said wearily, "but there's one thing I want you to do. Feeling against the bank was running pretty high yesterday. Dunning has convinced most people that Bonham's finished and we're to blame because the bank loaned us so much."

"That's why he'll be so damned mad when his scheme misses. He'll come bustling out here with his outfit."

Peg waved his words aside. "I'll take care of him if he comes here. Right now your job is to save the bank. If you take Yuma Bill into town, you'll probably both get killed before the money gets to Bonham, so what I want you to do is to leave Yuma outside of Ganado while you ride in and look things over. He could stay at Salty Smith's cabin, if he don't mind getting a leg talked off."

"I'm supposed to be bullet bait. That it?"

"That's it," she said, "only it'll be Dunning who gets the bullet if I know you."

"Thanks for your confidence in my shooting eye, but Yuma Bill won't want to . . ."

"She's right," Yuma Bill said. "It'd sure be hell to get to town and then have something happen so Brit didn't get the dinero."

Kim shrugged. "We'll play it that way if you want to, but I ain't sure it's the smart way."

He moved to Peg who stood beside the stove and kissed

41

her, but he found little warmth in her lips. When he stepped back, she gave him a tight smile.

"You see how it is," Peg said. "I threw myself at you last night, and you threw me back."

"It wasn't that way," he said. "It's just that I've got to know you trust my judgment."

"I trust your judgment, but I'm still giving the orders."

"Then you'll always give them," he said angrily, "and I'd still be Mr. Peg Cody."

For a moment they faced each other, their wills clashing, and he sensed it would always be that way with them. Turning, he walked out of the house into the growing light. The air was cool and heavy with dampness. It would rain again that day.

Kim and Yuma Bill saddled by the murky light of a lantern, and when they rode past the house, Peg stood silhouetted in the doorway, a tall slight figure, her back very straight. A chill of sudden fear ran down Kim's spine as he thought this might be the last time he would see her. He lifted a hand and she waved back. Then he rode on, the dark sprawling shape of the ranch house falling behind.

They splashed across Ganado Creek, running smoothly here between low banks, and followed the twin ruts of the road toward Ganado. The sun had tipped up over the Continental Divide, its scarlet light touching the Dragon Peaks across the valley. Slowly it climbed higher until it had rolled back the last of the shadows and full daylight was upon them.

Neither spoke for a time. Then Yuma Bill said, "Good grass."

"Cow paradise," Kim said. "Too damned bad anybody has to fight over it."

"Who's to blame?"

Kim shrugged. "I ain't paid to pass judgment, but if I was, I'd say old Sam Cody got his share of it. Peg's trying to hold what he left her."

"You'll find the blood of little men on every range like this," Yuma Bill said somberly. "And sooner or later you'll find the blood of more little men like Shorty Avis on the mesa. I never saw it fail. Greed begets greed. You're on the wrong side, boy."

"There's no right side," Kim said.

They rode in silence again, the level valley sweeping away all around them. Once Kim hipped around in his saddle and looked eastward to the series of benches that rose, step-like, toward the slick-rock rim that swung in a wide circle around the east side of the valley. Somewhere below that rim was Shorty Avis and his handful of cows, living in fear of Dutch Heinz's return.

Kim thought of Rocky Avis and what she had done for him and Yuma Bill the day before. He turned back, glancing at the little man's weathered face as he thought of his words, "You'll find the blood of more little men like Shorty Avis on the mesa." And discontent became a burning bitterness in Kim Logan.

"You hear anybody ride out last night?" Yuma asked suddenly.

"No. I didn't go to sleep for a while, and after I did, I didn't hear nothing. Why?"

"I did."

"You were dreaming. Nobody around but Peg."

Yuma Bill nodded. "That's just what I was thinking."

"But hell, she wouldn't . . ." Kim stopped. The little man was staring at the willow-lined, twisting course of Pass Creek, his leathery face very thoughtful. "Maybe she couldn't sleep and took a ride."

"She don't make a habit of it, does she?"

"No." Shrugging, Kim let it go at that, and pointed to the cluster of buildings ahead of them. "That's Ganado yonder."

Yuma Bill lifted himself in his stirrups, staring at the town. A church spire pointed skyward; a weathered brick building stood to the right of the church. Yuma asked, "What's that brick building?"

"Courthouse. Ganado is half cow town and half ghost town. The mining boom made it, and the old timers figured they'd have the biggest city in Colorado, so they built a courthouse that'd be fit and proper."

"Mines wear out?"

Kim nodded. "Nothing lasts, I reckon."

"Some things do. You just ain't found 'em yet."

"Preaching again," Kim said irritably.

Yuma Bill shook his head. "Just talking." His craggy face softened as a grin worked across his mouth. "I was the same when I was your age, full of sass and vinegar and never thinking past the next glass of whiskey or the next gal I was gonna kiss. Them are the things that don't last."

"What does?"

"No use me telling you. Every man has got to find 'em out for hisself." He swung a hand in a sweeping gesture. "I can't help wondering why you don't get your own outfit. More grass here than two outfits can use. Or if there ain't, go back where Avis is. He's up purty high, but there's plenty of range."

"That would have been a good idea twenty years ago, when a man with a rope and a running iron could get a start, but folks kind o' frown on them antics now."

"You can borrow."

43

"Where?"

"From the bank."

"And everything I'd make would go to Bonham for interest." Kim shook his head. "I never thought much about it until I got here with ten dollars in my pocket. Then I got to thinking. That started me to saving. First time in my life, but it's mighty slow."

"How much have you got?"

"A little over a thousand."

Yuma Bill nodded, apparently surprised that Kim had saved that much. He said, "Let's swing over to the cabin. I'll wait out here for half an hour or so. If you don't come shagging back, I'll trail along into town."

They could see the cabin now, a low long structure on the east bank of the creek. As they reined toward it, Kim said, "I don't cotton to this idea much, even if it is Peg's."

"Just one reason I do. It's to her interest that we get this dinero to the bank."

Kim said nothing more until they reached the cabin, Kim's eyes searching the willows that crowded the creek. He said, "Looks like Salty's gone. If he ain't in town, he's usually fishing."

"Who is he?"

"An old Civil War vet. Been here for years. Made one of the first strikes and lost everything over a poker table. Now he's living here just waiting to die." Kim stepped down. "I'll see if he's inside."

There was no answer to Kim's knock. He pushed the door open and looked in. The cabin was empty, the smell of it an insult to Kim's nostrils. He stepped out, closing the door. "You can go in if you want to. Smith wouldn't care. Right friendly old cuss when he ain't drunk, but he ain't what you'd call clean. The air's better out here."

"I'd just as soon sit in the willows. Might skip a rock or two across the creek." Yuma Bill glanced at his watch. "Getting along toward nine. You high tail into town and take this box to the bank. Dunning'll be looking for me. He won't figure on you having it."

"I don't like the idea. Damn it, I said I'd deliver you and your . . ."

Yuma Bill made an impatient gesture toward town. "Go on now. There's forty thousand in that box. I'm packing another ten in my money belt. I aimed to give all of it to Brit, but coming across the grass just now, I got a sudden hankering to go into the cattle business." He winked. "With a hairpin named Kim Logan."

Kim's mouth sagged open. "Why . . . you . . ."

Yuma Bill laughed. "Pull your eyes back inside your head.

44

You dust along. We'll be needing that bank one of these days, you and me."

"You know what we'll be into?" Kim demanded. "We'll be fighting Peg and Dunning both."

"All right. We'll fight 'em. Don't strike me that you're the kind of huckleberry who'd be afraid . . ."

"I ain't. I just didn't figure you'd want to buy a war of your own."

"I've bought one already. So have you. Let's say I want to sow some good seeds. Been a hell of a lot of weeds planted in these parts. Now take this box and move, or hod dang it, you'll be too late."

Shrugging, Kim took the box and stepped into the saddle. "Keep your eyes peeled."

Kim reined his buckskin around and touched him up, leaving the little man sitting his saddle in front of the cabin, his weathered face very thoughtful. As Kim rode away, he wondered what sort of past Yuma Bill had behind him, a past that had molded him into the kind of man who would travel halfway across the state with a fortune in a shoe box, his sole purpose that of repaying an old debt to a banker who had once helped him.

Ganado lay just ahead, false-fronted business buildings crowding Main Street, many of them deserted now, and dwellings, decorated with gingerbread and carved bargeboards and surrounded by picket fences with their carved corner posts. Most of the houses were empty; all were weathered to a dingy gray, their paint long gone, the fences needed repair, and the bulk of the boardwalks were splintered and grown up with weeds. A sort of genteel decay lay upon the town as if it had one eye upon its splendid past, the other closed to the future.

Kim reached the south end of Main Street when Rocky Avis appeared from a livery stable and rode toward him. It was a moment before she saw who he was, and when she did, she brought her horse to a gallop, waving at him to hurry.

When he came alongside her, she cried, "You're mighty slow. Where's Yuma Bill?"

"He's laying low at Smith's cabin till I see how things stack up. I've got his box."

"Then get a move on. It's almost time for Brit to open up, and there's a line waiting."

"Then they're gonna get a surprise. Come on and help me laugh in their faces."

Kim cracked steel to his buckskin and swept on down the street to the bank. He reined up and tied, eyes sweeping the line of grim-faced men. Some were little ranchers from Dunning's side of the valley, the small fry dependent upon HD just as Shorty Avis and his neighbors were dependent upon Clawhammer.

It was the others who brought a quick blaze of temper to Kim, townsmen who had no part in the feud, men who should be supporting Bonham: Doc Frazee, Fred Galt who owned the Mercantile, Luke Haines the barber, and a dozen more. Sheriff Ed Lane was in the line, a bald man who gave Kim a small nod, tongued his quid to the other side of his mouth, and turned his eyes away.

"What the hell you boys doing here?" Kim demanded.

"What does it look like?" Galt asked.

"Waiting for breakfast," Kim jeered. "Why don't you go home and eat?"

Doc Frazee, wearing a Prince Albert that had once been black and now was faded to a sort of dingy green, glared at Kim. "We'll go home when we get our money, and don't think you can stop us. Bonham wouldn't have got in this fix if he hadn't loaned our money to Clawhammer."

"That's right," Luke Haines cried in his shrill voice. "Just 'cause you're a tough hand working for Clawhammer don't mean you can change our minds."

Galt, the first man in the line, looked at his watch. He was a nervous man given to stomach trouble. Now he shoved his watch back into his pocket and began pounding on the door. "Nine o'clock, Bonham. Open up, damn it. Open up."

Others crowded against Galt, adding their voices to his until the words, "Open up, open up," became a sullen threatening rumble.

Kim could have showed them the money in the box; he could have said there was plenty to pay them and more, but he did neither. This was a selfish, senseless thing, a crime being committed by common men who thought they had their share of ordinary decency. It might have been forgivable in a man like Hank Dunning who pretended to be no better than he was; it was not forgivable in these townsmen.

Drawing his gun, Kim fired a shot over their heads. They faced him, bitter sullen men who had been swept by mob hysteria past the point where they were capable of honest reasoning.

"Do that again, Logan," the sheriff bawled, "and I'll throw you into the jug for disturbing the peace."

"Try it, Ed," Kim invited.

Lane looked away, jaws working steadily on his quid, a politician who had carried the star for ten years because he was a master at bowing to the right man. After Sam Cody had died, Dunning had been the man. It was common gossip on Pass Creek that every HD man had voted five times at the last election.

46

"What's the matter with you?" Galt demanded. "This ain't none of your put in."

"Now maybe it is," Kim said. "I've got some money in this bank, maybe, more than most of you boys, but I ain't asking for it. I figure the bank's sound."

"I don't," Galt flung back. "I ain't taking any chances."

"Are you trying to bust Bonham?"

"All I want is my dinero," Galt said doggedly.

"And you'll get it because you're first in line," Kim said, "but you don't give a damn about the boys behind you. You're a two-bit, selfish, stingy, money-loving son."

There was a crowding up from the tail of the line, men ramming and elbowing as their bitter voices rose in a menacing roar. Galt threw a quick look behind him, wizened face flooded with sudden fear.

Lane, the fourth man in the line, drew his gun and waved it at the ones behind him. "Order now, boys. Keep your places. Every man will have his turn."

They quieted, and Kim asked, "What time did you get here this morning, Fred?"

"None of your damned business!" the storeman screamed.

A rancher far back in the line said, "He was here at dawn. We had to do chores and ride in after that, so we couldn't get here that soon."

"Logan's just fixed to make trouble, Ed," Luke Haines said bitterly. "Run him in."

But Lane stood motionless, chewing steadily, eyes pinned on something down the street. Kim laughed, a contemptuous sound that ripped the last shred of dignity from the man.

"You poor damned fools," Kim flung at them. "You're doing Dunning's dirty work, and you ain't smart enough to know it." He looked back along the line, watching them stir and shift, boot heels scraping on the broken boards of the walk. He asked, "Where is Dunning?"

"Inside," Doc Frazee said. "Talking to Bonham."

"Listen now, you chuckle-heads," Kim shouted. "This ain't just my fight. Or Clawhammer's. It belongs to all of you. You've bowed and scraped to Dunning until you've forgotten you were men. You'll get your money if you want it, but you don't need it. and when you see that the bank's safe, you'll beg Bonham to take it back."

But they didn't stir. They stared at him defiantly, saying nothing, the men in the back of the line still pressing forward so that the ones in front were jammed hard against the door.

"I want to look at your ugly mugs in about ten minutes," Kim went on. "If you're worth a damn, you'll get down on your knees to Brit Bonham. Then you'll go tell Dunning to crawl under a rock where he belongs."

Without another word, Kim bulled his way through the line, knocking Luke Haines flat on his face, and stalked around the corner to the back door of the bank. It was locked. He looked through the window, saw Bonham sitting at his desk, head bowed. Dunning sat across from him, hawk-nosed face barren of expression.

Kim tapped on the window. When Bonham turned to look at him, he shouted, "Let me in, Brit. I've got something for you."

Bonham jumped up. Dunning said something that Kim couldn't hear, but Bonham shook his head and running to the door, turned the key and pulled the door open. Kim stepped in, his eyes locking with Dunning's. He said, "Hank, I've waited a long time for this. You're licked."

Dunning rose. He was a tall man, taller even than Kim, and now he seemed to be looking down, very confident. Quite casually he brought a hand to his face and scratched his great beak of a nose. He said, "I reckon not, Logan."

Kim walked to the desk and laid the box down. There, on the scarred walnut, were Peg Cody's notes. Bonham dropped into his swivel chair, faded eyes pinned on Kim's face. He asked hoarsely, "Did you see Yuma Bill?"

"I saw him." Kim slashed the cord that was around the box. "Funny thing, Brit. I've learned more about human nature since I met Yuma Bill than I'd learned in ten years before. It takes a pretty good man to have a friend like him." Kim lifted the lid from the box. "Better open up, Brit. There's a few boys outside who seem to want some cash money this morning."

CHAPTER 8

~~~~~~

POWDER FLAME

BONHAM cried out, a strained hoarse sound that a man would make who has lost all hope and then, unexpectedly, finds it again. He grabbed the box and ran out of his office into the bank, shouting, "Charlie, open up. We'll pay 'em right down to the last nickel."

Kim backed away from Dunning, hoping that this would be the moment he had long sought when Hank Dunning would go for his gun. Then he saw it was not. Dunning brushed at a lock of rebellious hair, dark eyes probing Kim with cool insolence. Kim had never seen him excited; he had never seen him hurry in anything he did. Now Dunning said, very deliberately, "Still lucky, Logan."

"Yesterday you sent Phil Martin and some of your boys across the creek after me. I reckon that opens the ball, don't it?"

Dunning shook his head. "Not today it don't."

"I don't cotton to the notion of playing coyote to your hounds. Let's finish it."

Again Dunning shook his head. "I never swap smoke with a hired hand." He walked past Kim and went into the street.

For a moment Kim stood staring after the big man until he disappeared around the corner. Then he turned and followed Bonham into the bank.

The teller, old Charlie Bemis, had unlocked the front door, but for a moment he was unable to get it open, so tightly were the men in front jammed against it. When he did, Fred Galt sprawled on his face, jumped up and lunged on across the room to the teller's wicket.

"I'm cleaning out my deposit," Galt yelled. "Every damned cent. You hear, Bonham?"

"I hear quite well, Fred," the banker said, very casually as if this were an ordinary occasion. "You'll get every cent as soon as Charlie looks up your balance."

Galt stood leaning against the counter, his bulging eyes fixed on the piles of currency that were stacked on a table beyond the teller's wicket. The others peered over his shoulder, Doc Frazee and Luke Haines and the rest. The silence was unexpected and strange, the shocked silence of men so stunned they were incapable of speech.

Then Haines let out a shrill squall. "Hell, he's got enough dinero on that table to buy the Denver mint. Look at it, Fred."

That broke the tension. They stormed forward, trying to get a closer look at this money they had not believed was here, jamming and shoving and cursing. There was no line at all now; the smaller men were pushed back. A rancher cried out in pain, screaming for somebody to get off his corns. The sheriff got an elbow into his stomach that knocked his wind out of him. He reeled away from the others and fell slack against the wall, struggling for breath.

Charlie Bemis called, "Fred's got a balance of $3,298.52."

"Be sure he gets that fifty-two cents," Kim said contemptuously.

"I certainly will." Bonham picked up a wad of greenbacks and counted out Galt's money. "There you are, Fred. Three thousand and two hundred." He dipped into a drawer. "I'll let you have the rest in gold and silver, except for the two pennies."

49

"Two-penny Galt," Kim jeered.

"Say, that's a good handle for him." A rancher slapped his leg, roaring with laughter. "Two-penny! Yes sir, that sure fits Galt."

Red-faced, Galt scooped up his money and pushed his way through the crowd. "Don't call me that, Rushmore, or I'll cut off your credit."

The rancher thumbed his nose at Galt. "To hell with you. We've needed a new store for a long time in this burg, Two-penny."

"What are you gonna do with that dinero, Two-penny?" Kim demanded. "Gonna lock it up in that cracker box of a safe of yours?"

Galt fled. Doc Frazee was staring at the currency through the teller's window, his bony face thoughtful. He said, "Boys, where'd we get the notion this bank wasn't sound?"

"Dunning," a rancher said. "You know that. He passed the word out that we had to be here today and ask for our money, or we'd have a hell of a hard time hanging on to our spreads."

"Tell 'em, Brit," Kim said. "Go on. Tell 'em so they'll know what caliber Hank Dunning is."

Bonham straightened, the corners of his mouth working. "Peg Cody borrowed thirty thousand from me to restock Clawhammer range. She's got five hundred head of prime steers she aims to sell in Durango this fall. That'll give her enough to pay the interest she owes me and maybe take up a few of the notes. Dunning wanted them notes. He was in my office just now offering me ten thousand for them."

"Why, the damned thieving crook," Luke Haines spluttered. "He aimed to bust Clawhammer."

"No doubt about it," Bonham said. "This bank is good. You boys ought to know that. I've got enough cash for ordinary business, but you'd have made me close my doors today if Kim hadn't fetched a chunk of money from a friend of mine who came in on the stage yesterday. Now if any of you want your deposits, you can sure have 'em. Just remember one thing. I don't want your business after today."

Doc Frazee pulled at his goatee, grinning as abashedly as a boy caught at a cookie jar. "Well, Brit, I haven't got a real good place to put my money if I had it. Reckon I'll just leave it here where it'll be safe."

"Me too," Haines cried.

"You boys ought to go take a look at yourselves," Kim said. "I wish I had your pictures right now. They'd be handy to look at if you forget what kind of ears a jackass has got."

Doc Frazee felt of his, grinning shamefacedly. "Pretty damned long, ain't they?" He moved away from the window to where Kim stood behind the gate at the end of the counter. "Say, you and the HD boys must have had quite a tussle."

"Burned a little powder, all right," Kim said.

"They rode in late yesterday," Frazee said, "wanting me to patch 'em up and they sure needed it. Tonto Miles was the only one who didn't. Martin's got a busted left arm, and that young Ernie Deal is gonna have a hard time making it. Got a slug in his brisket." Frazee lifted a bushy brow, hesitated, and then asked, "What started it?"

"They jumped us," Kim said shortly.

Frazee did not press the question. Shrugging, he turned away. "Well, Luke, let's go see how your wife's making out. You'll be a father before noon, or I miss my guess."

The medico walked out, Haines trailing behind him. The rest followed, abashed and silent. Bonham rubbed his face with trembling hands and dropped into a chair. "Put the money in the safe, Charlie." He brought his gaze to Kim. "Where'd you leave Yuma?"

"At Smith's cabin. We stayed the night at Clawhammer. When we left this morning, Peg allowed that Dunning might have a trap set up. She said for me to come in and see how things stacked up. Then Yuma got the notion I'd better fetch the box to you. Dunning wouldn't figure on me having it."

"He didn't," Bonham said. "No sir, he didn't. Have any trouble yesterday?"

Kim told him what had happened, adding, "You know, Brit, I've never been one to count on another man to pull my irons out of the fire. I didn't really figure Yuma Bill would be on that stage, but Peg said I'd better find out. Well, he was there all right."

"I gave him a little help once a long time ago. I knew he'd be there unless something happened." The banker rose. "Come on back, Kim."

Bonham walked to his private office, a tired, stoop-shouldered old man. He sat down behind his desk, motioning for Kim to take the other chair, and then picking up Peg's notes, stacked them neatly.

"I've been here a long time," Bonham said. "I've seen this town boom and I've seen it rot. I had the first bank here, and the last. I could have been a rich man if I'd used my money like some did, but I always had the notion that I'd live longer and die happier if I mixed a little justice with the banking business." He made a gesture toward the street. "But look what it got me. Just let somebody start some talk and they want their money."

"Well, I guess you sowed the right seeds," Kim said, "or Yuma Bill wouldn't have been on that stage."

51

Bonham started to fill his pipe. He stopped, glancing up at Kim. "Yuma still talking about sowing seeds?"

Kim nodded. "I told him he oughtta get a pulpit."

Bonham dribbled tobacco into his pipe and tamped it down. "No, he don't need a pulpit. You know, there was a time when he was the meanest, orneriest son of Cain who ever toted a gun. Now he's a different man. Call it a miracle if you want to, or just come out and call me a liar, but I seen it happen."

Kim waited, watching the banker light his pipe and blow out great clouds of smoke. There was more to the story, but he saw that Bonham was not of a mind to tell it now. He motioned to the notes. "How close did Dunning come to getting them?"

"Damned close." Bonham chewed on his pipestem, eyes filled with misery. "So close that I'm ashamed of myself. It was that or go bust. After being in the banking business for thirty years, well, I was reaching for any straw I could see."

"It would have finished Peg," Kim said morosely. "I don't savvy it, Brit. Dunning don't strike me as being the kind of a hairpin who'd figure out a sneak deal like this."

Bonham puffed for a moment. Then he said, troubled, "There's something that ain't right, but I can't put my finger on it. Just a feeling I get sometimes. Now old Sam was the sort who kicked everybody out of his way. He didn't have a friend in the valley except old Limpy and Dutch Heinz. When Sam was alive, Dunning behaved. He was afraid of Sam and Sam was a little afraid of him, I reckon. Then after he died, Dunning decided he'd start pushing."

Kim rose. "Well, might as well ride out and tell Yuma that everything's all right."

"I'll ride along." Bonham reached for his hat. "Been a long time since I saw old Yuma."

"Kim." It was Rocky Avis. "Kim, you here?"

"He's talking to Brit," Charlie Bemis told her.

Kim wheeled out of Bonham's office. Rocky stood in front of the teller's window, her face paler than Kim had ever seen it before. He asked, "What's up?"

She pushed open the gate at the end of the counter. He had always thought of her as a steady, capable girl, the kind who belonged to this wild land in which she lived. Now he saw the terror that was in her dark eyes; he sensed that she was close to being hysterical.

"Tonto Miles." She gripped Kim's arms. "He's been in the Belle Union all morning. Now he's out in front talking to Ed Lane. He says he'll kill you the minute you come out of the bank."

A deep satisfaction filled Kim as he considered this. It was

Dunning he wanted, not Miles, but a fight with Miles might force Dunning. Kim said, "Tonto can try, Rocky. That's all."

"But Lane says he'll jail both of you if you start anything."

"If we're both alive." Kim shrugged. "But if I know Ed, he's just talking through his hat."

"He's Dunning's man. It's a trap. You can't go out there, Kim."

Bonham had come up. He nodded, saying, "Rocky's right. Up till now you've just been a gnat buzzing in Dunning's ear, but when you knocked the bottom out of his scheme, you fixed it so he's got to get you, come hell or high water."

"I'll bring your horse around to the back," Rocky urged. "You've got to get out of town."

He shook his head, giving her a tight smile. "You've been in this country long enough to know I can't do that."

"No sense getting yourself killed for nothing," Bonham said in exasperation. "Get back to Clawhammer and fetch Heinz and his boys in. You're gonna have a finish fight sooner or later."

"Peg don't see that," Kim said. "She says she hired my gun, and it's time I was earning my pay."

"Why, she knows . . ." Bonham stopped, suddenly thoughtful. "I wonder."

"You wonder what?"

He shook his head. "Nothing. Just wool gathering."

Kim stepped away from Rocky and checked his gun. She moved in front of him, her small chin outthrust. The fear was gone from her now. She was angry, the same quick anger he had seen in her the day before when she had bitterly called him a "snake stomper."

"Kim, do you think Peg Cody is the kind of woman a man should die for?" Rocky demanded.

"Why, I hadn't thought of it just that way."

"Then start thinking. I told you she was a greedy woman."

"Well, we're all a little greedy, I reckon."

"But not like Peg Cody. Kim, you can't go out there and get yourself killed just for her hundred dollars a month."

"It's a little more than that, Rocky."

"No it isn't. Kim, can't you see how it is? There are some things that are worth dying for. I mean, things a man can believe in, but this is . . . is just throwing your life away for nothing."

He shook his head, looking down at her flaming face, and oddly enough, he thought of her as being pretty. Not in the way Peg Cody was. More like the beauty of a mountain storm. He put the thought from him. He said, "I've got a job to do."

"Let him go, Rocky," Bonham said.

Rocky whirled on him. "You men are all alike, but I thought you'd be different. He saved your bank for you . . ."

Kim moved past her, his .44 riding easily in its holster, and walked out of the bank into the sunlight. He stopped for a moment, letting his eyes get used to the glare. He heard Bonham say, "Charlie, get them Winchesters out of the closet." He would have a fair fight, and that was all a man who lived by the gun could ask.

Tonto Miles stood in front of the Belle Union, a burly man who had come to the valley after Kim had. Seeing Kim, he bawled, "I've been looking for you, Logan."

Ed Lane was standing beside Miles. Now he drifted away and disappeared. Kim moved along the walk until he was clear of the hitch pole, then stepped into the street, hands at his sides. Neither Dunning nor Martin were in sight. There had been other men on the boardwalk. Now they were gone.

Miles stepped off the walk and moved into the street, great head canted forward on massive shoulders. Suddenly, and it was the first time in his life that Kim had ever felt this way, he was tired of fighting.

A few minutes before Dunning had said he never swapped smoke with a hired hand. Kim Logan was that. No more. No less. Here they were, Tonto Miles and Kim Logan, hired hands, both of them, although the hope was in Kim that he was more than that to Peg Cody. Their deaths would settle nothing. Other men would be hired. He thought of the fellow who had fallen off the rim the afternoon before, a man who had made a bad bargain. Then the thoughts fled; this was no time for them if he wanted to live.

Slowly Kim and Tonto Miles moved into the street, tense, watchful. One measured step, then another, boots falling into the street dirt, still soft from yesterday's rain. Overhead the sun was a brilliant searing ball in a clear sky, sucking up moisture from a wet earth, the air heavy with the smell of it. From some vacant lot a bird began to sing, a sweet clear sound that beat against Kim's ears. A thought jarred him. It might be the prelude for his passage into eternity.

They were close, so close that Kim could see the purple veins in Miles' cheeks, the red flecks in his eyes. Then Miles made his draw. Warned by the down drop of the man's right shoulder, the quick flick of lips pulled tight against yellow teeth, Kim drove his right hand toward gun butt and swept it clear of leather. It was swift sure motion without waste, the perfect co-ordination of nerve and muscle that comes to a man only after long and honest practice.

The gun bucked in Kim's hand; powder flame made its brief stab of fire against the sun's glare. The roar of the shot ran along the street, deserted except for these two, the one who died and the one who lived. Then Kim stood alone, staring down at Tonto Miles who lay with his face in the dirt, right hand flung out beside his unfired gun. Then, and again it was a strange new feeling to Kim, a revulsion swept through him, a sort of sickness, and with it was a bitter hatred for Hank Dunning who had caused this.

Men boiled into the street, Doc Frazee in the lead, black bag in hand, the tails of his faded Prince Albert flying behind him. Kim looked back and saw Brit Bonham and Charlie Bemis standing in front of the bank, cocked Winchesters in their hands. Then he crossed the street, moving past the men knotted around Miles' body, and heard Frazee say, "Right through the heart. Never saw no better shooting."

Kim went into the saloon. He said, "Whiskey," hoping it would take the sour taste out of his mouth. Only then was he aware that he still held his gun at his side. He holstered it, eyeing the bartender who shoved a bottle and glass at him with the wariness of a man approaching a coiled rattlesnake. That, too, was grimly familiar. Kim was used to it, but after all these years, he still resented it.

They would remember him, these men who had watched from open doorways and windows with the sadistic pleasure of ancient Romans gathered in the Coliseum, and remembering it, they would be afraid of him. There had been a time when street fights were common occurrences in Ganado, but that had been years ago, and only a few like Doc Frazee and Brit Bonham would remember. There had long been talk of trouble between Clawhammer and the HD, bets had been placed as to when the first blood would be spilled. Now the day had come, and from this hour, Kim Logan would be a marked man.

He took his drink and set the glass back on the polished mahogany. He filled it again and let it stand, staring moodily at the amber liquid. No good. The sourness remained in him. Liquor could not take it from him.

Men came in. The batwings clapped shut, the sibilant sound reached Kim at the bar. He turned his head. Sheriff Ed Lane stood there, tobacco quid bulging one cheek. Johnny Naylor, the shotgun guard, stood behind him. Both were scared and showed it, Naylor so panicky he was close to bolting. Lane came on until he stood within ten feet of Kim. He said, trying hard to make a tough appearance, "Lay your gun on the bar, Logan. You're under arrest."

≈⊂⊂⊂⊂⊂⊂⊂⊂⊂⊂⊂⊂⊂⊂⊂⊂⊂⊂⊂⊂⊂⊂⊂⊂⊂⊂⊂⊂⊂⊂⊂⊂⊂⊂⊂⊂

CHAPTER 9

JAILED

FOR a moment Kim said nothing. He did not move. He stood with his left hand on the bar, right at his side within inches of gun butt, staring blankly at Lane as he mentally groped for an explanation. He said finally, "Say that over, Ed."

"You're under arrest," Lane repeated. "Put your gun on the bar and head for the door."

"You can't pull this off," Kim said. "A dozen men saw that fight. You know I couldn't duck it."

"I ain't arresting you for plugging Miles," Lane said, emboldened by Kim's lack of resistance. "It's for stopping the stage yesterday and taking a gent named Yuma Bill off it."

Kim's gaze swung to Johnny Naylor, anger stirring in him. "So you've sold out, too, Johnny. Your caliber is a damned sight smaller than I thought it was."

"I didn't sell out to nobody," Naylor cried. "I just ain't gonna let you get away with stopping the stage and taking a man off at point of a gun. You ain't that big, Logan."

"I didn't take him. He got out when I mentioned Brit Bonham. Remember?"

"Yeah, and you had a gun in your hand. Remember that?"

Kim shrugged. "If I hadn't, you'd have drilled me. I had to keep you quiet so I could talk to Yuma."

"You held a gun on us," Naylor said doggedly. "You scared hell out of us. That fat woman fainted. Might have died of heart failure. If we've got any law around here, it won't stand for it."

"We've got law all right," Lane said smugly, "and it don't stand for them kind of shenanigans. Now are you . . ."

"Oh hell! If I hadn't taken Yuma, some of Dunning's outfit would. He'd have been beefed by now and the bank would be busted."

"He wouldn't have been touched," Naylor said with malicious triumph. "We rolled into Ganado without no more trouble."

Doubts struck Kim then. He had not asked if the stage had been stopped again. He had been so sure it would be Dunning's move that he had not questioned it. He said, "You're lying, Johnny."

"I ain't neither. Ask the driver. Or the passengers. The

drummer's over at the hotel and that fat woman is Luke Haines' mother-in-law. She was coming to take care of Mrs. Haines. She's in Luke's house now. Go ask her."

"All right," Kim said, "but you still haven't got a charge against me, Ed. We stopped at Rocky Avis' place on our way down and she cooked dinner for us. She'll tell you Yuma wasn't no prisoner. You can't make kidnapping out of it."

"I'm making it kidnapping all right," Lane said doggedly. "I'll ask Rocky, but as long as Johnny sticks to his story, I've got to throw you into the jug."

Ed Lane was a poor excuse for a lawman. Still, Kim could not draw a gun on him. Killing a man like Tonto Miles was one thing; shooting the sheriff was quite another. Kim drew his gun and laid it on the bar. He walked toward the bat-wings, saying, "I won't be in long, Johnny. Not when Yuma Bill tells his story. Then you'd better get out of my way."

"Take more'n that to get you out of the jug," Naylor said, his terror gone now that Kim's gun was not in holster. "Butch told you Clawhammer wasn't big enough to save your hide."

"We'll see," Kim said, and pushed through the batwings.

Miles' body had been moved and the street was empty. Kim paused, wondering who would go to Clawhammer for him. Peg, he was sure, would arrange for bail and get him out as soon as she heard.

"Keep moving," Lane said. "Try anything and I'll plug you. Just anything."

Kim turned toward the courthouse, resentment smoldering in him. Lane did not need to keep the gun in his back, but it was like the man, now that Kim was unarmed. It gave him his chance to play big; he would relish telling Dunning how he had arrested and disarmed Kim Logan, the man who had killed Tonto Miles.

They moved slowly, Lane two paces behind Kim. They passed Luke Haines' barber shop, Galt's Mercantile, and when they reached Doc Frazee's drugstore, Kim heard running steps on the walk behind him. He turned. It was Rocky Avis and he saw at once that her temper was honed sharp again.

"Ed, what are you up to now?" Rocky demanded.

Lane stepped back so that he could watch both Kim and Rocky. He licked brown-stained lips, eyeing Rocky warily. "Don't you try none of your tricks. You're a wild cat all right, but my jail can hold wild cats along with gunmen."

Rocky stamped a foot, so angry that for a moment Kim thought she was going to slap Lane. "Why are you arresting him?"

"What's that to you?"

"Plenty. You put out some talk about arresting anybody who got into a gun fight in Ganado, but you can't make it stick and you know it."

"I'll make this stick. He's arrested for kidnapping a feller named Yuma Bill. Now git back . . ."

"Why, you pumpkin-headed fool! Yuma Bill wasn't kidnapped. They stopped at my place and I cooked dinner for them. I saw how it was."

"Johnny Naylor says different. Now git out of the way, Rocky, or so help me, I'll . . ."

"Johnny Naylor, is it? We'll see about that."

Rocky whirled and started back along the walk. Kim called, "Rocky, wait." She turned back, standing motionless as if poised for flight. "Ride out to Clawhammer and tell Peg what happened. She'll get me out."

Rocky stared at him blankly for a moment before she seemed to understand what he had said. Then she flared, "You don't need your precious Peg. I'll fix this." Again she whirled and this time Kim let her go.

"She ain't so big," Lane said with his usual smugness. "Move along."

The brick courthouse stood at the end of the block, Ganado's chief reminder of the glory that was past. Only the first story was used. The other two were empty, most of their windows knocked out by Ganado's stone-throwing boys. In recent years they had been boarded up, giving the building the same appearance of decay that was typical of the town.

Kim pulled the front door open, said, "Some oil would stop that squeak," and went on down the dark hall to Lane's office, floor boards squealing dismally under his feet. He stood motionless beside the desk while the sheriff threw a cell door back and motioned with his head.

"Ain't had much business lately." Lane locked the door behind Kim. "Time it was picking up. A sheriff oughtta earn his salary, hadn't he?"

"Yeah. Dunning's money."

Lane turned to spit in the direction of the big brass spittoon at the end of his desk. He swung back, wiping a hand across his mouth. "Well now, you go ahead and talk ornery if you want to. Won't make me mad. Won't do you no good, neither."

Kim sat down on the bunk and rolled a smoke, paying no attention to Lane who stood staring at him a little uncertainly, apparently surprised that Kim was taking the arrest so calmly. He asked, "Hungry?"

"No."

Lane dropped Kim's gun into a drawer of his desk. He said, "I'll fetch you a meal from the hotel afore sundown," and walked down the hall, the squeal of the boards coming back to Kim. After that there was silence.

Kim had been in jail a few times, but never more than an hour or so, and never for anything more serious than cracking some local cowboy on the nose during a Saturday night free-for-all. This, he knew, could be serious. He smoked his cigarette down and rolled another, his hatred for Hank Dunning becoming a poison in him.

One thing was clear to Kim. Dunning was a more careful man than he had thought. He had rigged up one trap behind another so that if the first failed, there would be the second and then a third. He had not succeeded in buying Peg's notes, so he had tried to remove Kim by throwing a gunman at him. That had failed, but at least he had Kim in jail, and it was more than probable that he could swing enough influence to secure a conviction. Then he could move on Clawhammer without fear of serious opposition.

Kim thought briefly of Rocky Avis, wondering what she had in mind and having no real hope of her success. He should have asked Lane to send Brit Bonham to see him. Bonham, he was sure, would see that Peg heard what had happened.

Peg would get him out. He had no doubt of that. She needed him. He had every reason to think she loved him. Then he swore softly and rubbed his cigarette out. He had missed a bet last night because of a perverse notion that he had to prove to Peg what he could do before he asked her to marry him. He wouldn't pass up another chance if it came.

He heard steps in the hall, the floor squealed, and Kim got up from the cot and rattled the bars. He yelled, "Hey, you out there." There was no answer, but the steps kept coming, the floor boards squeaked just outside the sheriff's office. Then the door opened. Lane came in, red-faced and sullen. Johnny Naylor was behind him, then Rocky Avis and Naylor's wife Della. Naylor looked like a kid who has just been soundly threshed, Rocky was smiling, and Della had the appearance of a tornado with the cork pulled.

Without a word Lane unlocked the cell door and swung it back. He said sourly, "You're free. Naylor changed his story. Said the stage had already stopped and Yuma Bill got out 'cause he wanted to."

Kim walked out of the cell and crossing to Lane's desk, opened a drawer and took out his gun. He checked it and dropped it into holster, guessing that Della was the one who had pulled it off. She was Rocky's age and her best friend, coming from one of the small ranches on the mesa. Kim knew she often visited Rocky, and whenever Rocky stayed in town overnight, it was always with Della.

"What are you waiting on?" Rocky asked. "You like it in here?"

Kim grinned. "Can't say I do, but I'm a mite curious."

"I'll settle your curiosity right now," Della said sharply. "It's going to take some regular Sunday School living from Johnny to make me forget this. If we can't get along on his wages . . ."

"Now Della . . ." Naylor began.

"Don't Della me," she flung at him. "I wouldn't blame Kim if he blew your head off, but I've got a hunch I'm saving your life by telling him what you did. He was sore about your stopping the stage, Kim. Maybe he had a right to be, but he didn't have a right to take Dunning's hundred dollars and swear you into jail. Now he's swearing you out."

"A hundred dollars, was it?" Kim asked softly. "You lie cheap, Johnny."

"I didn't do no lying," Naylor muttered. "You did have a gun in your fist."

"But you didn't think to tell Ed about it until after Tonto Miles cashed in. That right?"

"Yeah, it's right," Naylor said sulkily.

"And you knew that Miles was going to make a try for me?"

Naylor looked at Kim defiantly. "I knew all right. He was sore 'cause you shot hell out of his bunch below the rim yesterday. Dunning claims you're fixing to pull this valley into the damnedest range war the country ever saw. If it takes killing you to stop it . . ."

"All right," Lane broke in. "No use of this palaver. Vamoose."

Della gripped Kim's arm. "Johnny got you into this, but now he's got you out. Not sore at him now, are you?"

"I can take care of myself," Naylor shouted, his pride outraged. "Del, you'd better stay out . . ."

"I ain't sore." Kim gave Della a sour grin. "Not much. Anyhow, you're too pretty to be a widow. Come on, Rocky."

They went down the hall, Rocky half running to keep up with Kim's long strides. She said, "I knew Della would fix Johnny. She doesn't like Dunning any more than I do. When Johnny started bragging about the hundred dollars he'd won at poker, Del guessed what had happened and she made him tell her."

"Wouldn't be hard to guess. Johnny's the worst poker player in the valley."

"Del tells him that, but Johnny doesn't think he's so bad. He keeps trying to show her that he's not as hopeless as she thinks he is."

They stepped into the sunlight, Kim taking a deep breath.

"You know, Rocky, good air is something you don't put the right price on till you're cooped up in a stinking jail for awhile."

"It's that way with a lot of things, I guess. What are you going to do now?"

"Go back to Clawhammer. Say, did Yuma Bill get into town?"

"Why, I don't know. I haven't seen him."

"Let's take a sashay out to Smith's cabin and see what's holding him up. You'll want to pick up your dad's horse anyhow."

"Kim." The girl gripped his arm. "Look."

He stared down the street, shocked into silence by what he saw. Hank Dunning and Phil Martin were riding into town from the south. Smith's cabin was in that direction. Dunning was leading the black horse that Kim had borrowed from Shorty Avis for Yuma Bill; a man was lashed belly-down across the saddle.

Kim ran toward them, a terrible fear crowding him. Yuma Bill was dead! He was too far away to recognize the man tied in the saddle; he could not tell at this distance whether the man was dead, but he knew. He should never have left Yuma Bill alone.

Other men were boiling into the street. Someone shouted, "Another killing." By the time Kim and Rocky reached Galt's Mercantile, Dunning had reined up in the middle of the street, motioning for Martin to stop. Men crowded around them, asking questions, but for a moment Dunning ignored them. Kim shouldered through the crowd, his eyes making certain what had been in his mind. The man tied across the saddle was Yuma Bill and he was dead.

Brit Bonham was beside Kim, shaking his shoulder. "It's Yuma Bill, isn't it? It is Yuma Bill."

Kim backed away, nodding. He put his gaze on Dunning who was staring down at him, black eyes somber and probing. Kim asked, "You killed him, Dunning?"

Fury swelled the big man's chest. He swore, motioning to Ed Lane who had come up behind Kim. "Hear that, Sheriff? This killing thief wants to know if I done it."

"Did you?" Kim asked hoarsely.

"Tell 'em what you saw, Phil," Dunning ordered.

Martin was a sick man. His left arm was in a sling; his broad face was gray, mirroring the suffering that was in him. Now he licked dry lips, right hand clutching the saddle horn as if it was an effort to remain upright.

"I was coming into town to have Doc look at my arm," Martin said slowly. "Logan and another hombre was riding in from the southeast. From Clawhammer, I reckon. They stopped at Smith's cabin. They got down and Logan opened the door. He looked in, then he turns around and shoots the other fellow. He grabs the dead man's money belt and lights out for town."

"You've got it easy, Ed," Dunning said. "It ain't often you've got an eyewitness to a murder."

Kim stood motionless, stunned by Martin's story. He heard the sullen mutter of the crowd, heard Fred Galt shout, "That's why he was so high and mighty about us getting our money out of the bank. He already had his nest feathered."

"It's a lie," Rocky cried. "I met Kim on his way to town this morning . . ."

"But you didn't see him at Smith's cabin, did you?" Dunning demanded. "You didn't see 'em from the time they stopped at Smith's cabin till Logan left, did you?"

"No, but . . ."

"All right, Ed," Dunning said. "This girl don't know nothing about it. Phil does because he saw it."

Kim stepped back, hand dropping to gun butt. It was a rigged play, smart and brutal, another trick lined up behind the others that had failed.

"Take it easy, Logan." Lane's gun rammed against Kim's back. "That cell you left is empty and waiting." He lifted Kim's .44. "Back you go."

"Hold on," Kim shouted. "Martin's lying just like Rocky said. This man was alive when I left him. If I'd aimed to kill him, I'd have taken the dinero I fetched to the bank, and I'd have kept going."

"No," Dunning said. "You're too smart for that. Bonham told around that he had a friend coming with some money. It's my guess you spent the night at Clawhammer and Peg Cody knew what was in the box, but chances are she didn't know he was toting some more dinero in his money belt. You could take that and figger you was safe 'cause no one around here knew he had it on him."

"I saw what I saw," Martin said doggedly. "I'll swear to it if this killing son lives long enough to be tried."

"He won't," Galt bawled. "I'll donate the rope myself, and I'll put the loop on his neck."

Lane wheeled on the storekeeper, making a show of anger. "None of that talk, Fred. I never lost a prisoner out of my jail yet, and I ain't starting with Logan."

Bonham had stood like a man struck by paralysis. Only now did he seem to fully grasp what was happening. He gripped Lane's arm. "Listen, Ed. If you used your noggin you'd know that Martin's lying. Logan's been in town since nine this morning. Martin wouldn't have waited all this time to tell what he saw."

"I waited all right," Martin said. "I tried to get to town, but I couldn't make it. Fainted, I reckon. Fell out of my saddle anyway. Hank found me. I told him what I just told you." He stopped, swaying, and pitched headlong to the ground.

"Doc," Dunning called. "Take care of Phil."

Doc Frazee motioned to Galt and Johnny Naylor. "Tote Martin over to my office. Dunning, you take the body to my back room." He reared back, long face dark with anger. "But before you do it, there's one thing I want to say. When I first hit this here camp, it was wilder'n hell, but I never seen nothing like this for framing a man. It's too pat, Dunning, just too damned pat."

Turning, Frazee stalked across the street to his office, the tails of his faded Prince Albert flapping behind him. Lane said, "Move along, Logan."

"Get word to Peg, will you, Brit?" Kim asked, and when Bonham nodded, Kim winked at Rocky. "It's all right. I'll be out again by sundown. Ed's gonna be plumb discouraged locking me up."

Kim paced along the boardwalk to the courthouse, knowing it wasn't all right, not on a murder charge with Fred Galt hating him the way he did, and Dunning willing to oil men's throats with free whiskey in the Belle Union. Nothing more was needed to start a blood lusting mob toward the courthouse. Saner men like Brit Bonham and Doc Frazee would be pushed aside.

Kim reached the courthouse, Lane two paces behind, looking very smug and sure of himself. He asked, "Scared?"

"Some."

"You've got cause to be," Lane said with satisfaction.

The heavy outside door had been propped open. They went in and on down the length of the dark hall, floor boards squeaking dismally under their feet.

"Go right in," Lane said. "I left your cell open."

Kim obeyed, and for the second time that day the cell banged shut behind Kim.

CHAPTER 10

FOUR WALLS

A STRANGE uneasiness suddenly possessed Ed Lane. He dropped Kim's gun into a drawer and paced around the office for a few minutes, chewing nervously on a huge quid of tobacco. Finally he asked, "Anything you want, Logan?"

"No."

"Hungry yet?"

"No."

"Ain't et since breakfast, have you?"

"No."

"I'll go over to the hotel and have 'em cook you up a good meal. Anything special you want?"

"What are you trying to do, ease your conscience by giving a condemned man his last meal?"

Lane bristled. "You won't get your last meal till after you're legally tried and convicted, which same you will be. And don't say nothing about my conscience. I didn't take an old man off the stage and then plug him right here at the edge of town."

"Been smarter to have plugged him farther out, wouldn't it?"

"It sure would. Looks to me like you ain't as smart as Dunning allows you are."

"How come you didn't arrest Martin and his outfit for jumping me and Yuma Bill yesterday?"

"Nobody made no complaint," Lane said, turning sullen. "If I'd arrested anybody, it'd be you, jumping 'em like you done."

"So that's the way Martin tells it. How did he account for being on Clawhammer's side of the creek?"

"He didn't. They wasn't breaking no law, just riding like they was."

Lane wheeled and stepped out. The boards squeaked and were still. Silence then, tight and oppressive. Kim sat down on his bunk and rolled a smoke. He fired it and took a long drag, but there seemed to be no taste to it. He ground it out under a boot toe, got up and paced the length of his cell, physically sick. In the few hours he had known Yuma Bill, he had learned to respect him as he had respected few men in his short turbulent life.

Death was not a new thing to Kim. Like most men who live by the gun, the knowledge that death is the natural and inevitable destiny for every human was never fully absent from his mind. But these last hours had changed him as surely as a dam diverts a flowing stream, and it had been Yuma Bill who had done the changing, a Yuma Bill who would have made himself felt in the entire valley if he had lived. Now Kim was haunted by the thought that he was at least partly to blame for the little man's death.

There was another thing, too, that added to his misery. As far back as he could remember, he had wanted to own a ranch, a natural ambition for a man who had been raised in the cattle country. Until he had come to Pass Creek Valley, he had never really planned beyond the next day. As Yuma Bill had said, he had been satisfied to think about a glass of whiskey, a girl to kiss, the transient things which had no lasting qualities.

After he had come to the valley, change had begun to work in him. Here was a country big enough for a dozen ranches, but there were just the two with the threat of war between them. It had been that threat which was largely responsible for keeping other cowmen out and for holding the little outfits back on the poorer graze of the mesa.

Then Yuma Bill had proposed a partnership. It had been there, right at his finger tips, the thing he wanted more than anything else. Now it was snatched away. He was back where he had started from, a hired gun hand with a thousand dollars in the bank, accused of murdering the very man who had promised to turn a dream into reality.

Later, hours later it seemed to Kim, Lane brought Brit Bonham to his cell. The banker was wearing a slicker. He said, "Rain's about here."

Kim had not been aware of the gathering storm. He said, "Won't last long," and watched Lane search Bonham for a gun, saying in a surly voice that he wasn't taking any chances. He drifted back to his desk and stood there, watching, giving Kim and Bonham a chance to talk. It was a courtesy Kim had not expected from him.

"I sent a man to Clawhammer," Bonham said. "He oughtta be back in another hour or so. If Peg's got any sense, she'll send her boys in and yank you out of here before it's too late."

"I won't run," Kim said sharply. "Running convicts a man if nothing else does."

"You can't prove your innocence locked up here," Bonham snapped. "Use your head, boy. Dunning's buying free drinks in the Belle Union right now. He's bent on getting rid of you, and a rope is a cheap way to do the job."

"Must be some men in town who don't figure the way he does," Kim said.

Bonham glanced at the sheriff and brought his eyes back to Kim. "Sure. Me and Doc and Charlie Bemis. Maybe one or two more. Or supposing you stand trial? What chance have you got against Martin's testimony." Bonham shook his head. "We've got to bust you out someway."

Kim gripped the bars. "I've been wondering about a couple of things. Was Dunning in town when me and Tonto Miles tangled?"

"Dunno. I'll find out."

"And what about old Salty Smith?"

"I've been wondering that myself," Bonham said. "I don't think he's been around town today."

"Then he'd be fishing."

Bonham nodded, considering this. "He never fishes downstream. Usually he goes about a mile up the creek and fishes back down. Thick as them willows are, he could have been in sight of his cabin when it happened and seen the whole thing."

"He knows Dunning and Martin," Kim said. "If he saw it, he'd be afraid to talk."

"I'll ride out there. He'll talk to me."

Bonham swung away from the bars. Lane asked, "Done?"

"Yeah, except for one question, Ed. It's a pretty poor stick of a sheriff who don't think of justice first. You ain't gonna be proud of yourself if you hang the wrong man."

"What're you getting at?"

"I've been wondering what you'd do if you had proof that Martin or Dunning shot Yuma Bill?"

Lane snorted. "Hell, I've got proof that Logan done it. That's all I need."

"A good lawman looks a little deeper than what's throwed on top for him to see. It's like Doc said. This thing is too pat."

"Makes sense," Lane said doggedly. "Anyhow, it's up to the jury, not me."

"Maybe it'll never go to a jury."

Lane chewed hard on his quid, face turning red. He burst out, "Damn it, Brit, nobody's gonna take Logan out of here. You hear? Nobody."

"They'll try, and I can't see you being man enough to die bucking a lynch mob. There's another thing you'd better be thinking on. If Kim killed Yuma Bill, he done it before nine this morning. That right?"

"Yeah, but . . ."

"Doc says he hasn't been dead that long." Bonham turned

66

back to Kim. "Your horse is in the stable. He'll be taken care of." He swung around and went out.

For a long moment Lane stood motionless. Then he muttered, "Aw, hell, Doc couldn't tell," and stomped out after Bonham.

It began to rain in sudden violence much as the storm had come the day before. Kim stood up on his cot and looked out of the one small window. This was the shabbiest and most decayed part of a decaying town. Log cabins scattered haphazardly about, doors half off their hinges, roofs falling in, yards and streets grown high with weeds. Now, for one brief moment, the rain drew a silver curtain across this tawdry scene.

Kim got down, futility weighing heavily upon him. He had always been a man to depend upon himself and his gun, confident of his strength and speed. Now, for the first time that he could remember, he was completely trapped. There was no way out, no way by which he could help himself. There were those who wanted to help him, but if they did, they would risk their lives, and that was something he did not want.

He rolled a cigarette and smoked it, seeing the situation with stark clarity. His one hope lay in old Salty Smith, but in spite of what Bonham had said, the hope at best was a slim one.

At first he had expected help from Peg. Now, with the slow minutes dragging by, he realized that Peg could not help him, that his trust in her was as empty of real value as a pocketful of fool's gold. Even if she was willing to bring her crew down from the high country, Dutch Heinz would refuse to do anything.

Then a new fear clutched Kim. This might have been pulled off by Dunning to lure Clawhammer men away from the cattle and leave them unguarded. He pushed the thought from his mind at once. One thing overshadowed everything else in Peg's mind, the safety of her herd. She would not order her men to leave her cattle whether Kim Logan's neck was stretched or not.

The storm moved on. Thunder was softened by distance, the only lightning was that along the horizon. Kim knew how it would be outside: a hot clear sun, the heavy damp air, mud squishing under boot heels, the clean smell of a washed steaming earth. Those were things that a free man could see and feel.

A free man! Panicky, he jumped up and pounded the bars; he shouted and kicked, and then realizing what was happening to him, he dropped back on the cot, ashamed. He wasn't licked. A man had a chance as long as he was alive, but no one except Brit Bonham would gamble on that chance. Even

Rocky Avis hadn't come to see him. Not that he blamed her. She'd probably taken her father's black horse and headed for home. She'd already done enough for him. More than enough. More than he had any right to expect.

He clenched his fists and spread them and clenched them again. He got up and began pacing the floor, fighting the fear that beat at him. If he had any kind of a chance, he would run. They could think what they wanted to. As Bonham had said, he could not prove his innocence here. He might, if he was free.

Free! The word hammered at his mind like the rhythmical roll of distant drums. Free! Free! Free! Only a free man had strength and will and the capacity to fight. Here he was like a wild horse in a corral. Now he understood how a stallion felt, driven in from the high open mesas to have his great heart broken; he knew why a stallion would fight until he killed himself or broke a leg and had to be killed.

Then, and he was not aware just how or why, the queer feeling of panic began to die. He thought of Peg who had gambled on him for protection just as she had gambled on the future, borrowing every cent she could from Brit Bonham. He thought of Shorty Avis who hated him because he hated and feared Clawhammer, of Rocky who had helped him.

Then, and he felt as if a sharp blade had been driven through him, he thought of Yuma Bill who talked about planting good seeds. Kim had had a lifetime of freedom, but he had taken little of it to think. Now he had time. He sat quietly on his cot, his mind on Yuma Bill, and he realized that he had respected the little man for a very simple reason. Yuma Bill had lived the life he'd talked. There could be no other reason for his coming here to help Brit Bonham. That was what he had meant when he'd said that a man must find the things that lasted. He had found them, Kim Logan never had.

It was close to evening when Ed Lane came with his meal: hot coffee, a thick steak, fried potatoes, and biscuits, the kind of meal Kim would have ordered if he had been in the hotel dining room. He said, "Thanks, Ed."

"Thought you'd be getting a little lank," Lane said. "I told that China boy he'd better do a good job on that steak, or I'd have his pigtail."

Kim understood. Ed Lane knew what to expect tonight; he was not a man to die for an abstract principle called duty. As far as he was concerned, Kim Logan was a dead man swinging from a limb. By bringing this meal, Lane was easing his conscience. Later he would say he had done all he could.

When Kim finished, Lane took the plate, cup, and coffeepot. "Time to put the feed bag on myself," he said, and left the jail.

Silence again after the last board had squealed under Lane's feet, but it did not seem quite so oppressive now. Kim emptied his sack of Durham and smoked the last cigarette. The sun was almost down. He remembered how it was, the Dragon Peaks forming giant saw teeth against the western sky, the vivid sweep of scarlet sunset, shadows darkening the edge of the valley and slowly moving on across it.

The world could be a good place to live, but it was seldom that. There was a right and a wrong side to every human difference, but few sides were completely right or wrong. That was why there was so much trouble in the world, for it was natural that a man who had only a part of the right would think he had all of it.

Hank Dunning could probably make a case for himself. And old Sam Cody if he were still alive. Even back before that there were the gold seekers chasing the yellow floozy, greedy men too often without conscience. A man could not tell where it had started. Perhaps it had always been that way. Kim only knew he had been a part of it, using his gun and dealing in death for those who could pay.

He felt no pride in his past. He could not change anything he had done. The page was full. He rubbed out his cigarette, feeling none of the panic that had been in him earlier in the afternoon. He realized that these were the thoughts of a man facing death.

The light was very thin when Lane returned with Bonham. Again the lawman searched Bonham for a gun and stepped back so that they could talk.

"I found out a couple of things," Bonham said. "Dunning was in town until after you plugged Tonto Miles. Then he rode south. Mean anything?"

"Not much. How do you figure it?"

"Looks to me like maybe Martin was holding Yuma prisoner out there till Dunning told him what to do. They wanted the dinero Yuma had on him, and they wanted you out of the way without having to dry gulch you which might be a little dangerous for them."

Kim nodded. "Could have been that way all right."

"I was the cause of it," the banker said bitterly. "If I hadn't . . ."

"None of that," Kim cut in. "I can say the same thing about myself. My mistake was doing what Yuma wanted, but hell, it sounded reasonable. A man just can't foresee things like this."

"I reckon that's the way to look at it," Bonham agreed, "but it's pretty tough just the same."

"Smith?"

"I dunno. I spent half the afternoon on the creek. He might have been fishing. Couldn't tell. The rain probably washed out any sign there was before I got there. The only thing I'm sure of is that he ain't around now."

The last small hope was gone, but it was no more than Kim expected. He asked, "Peg?"

"She got my note," Bonham said heavily, "but I don't know what to expect. She just said 'Thanks,' gave the boy a dollar, and went back into the house."

"I guess that's it."

Kim gripped the bars, knuckles white, and he felt again the emptiness in his middle that made him want to scream and beat at the bars. He thought of men he had seen die with a rope on their necks. He had had a part in some of those hangings. At the time there had seemed to be no doubt of their guilt. Rustling! Horse stealing! Murder! Now he wondered. Most of the men who would have a part in lynching him would have no doubt of his guilt. Johnny Naylor. Luke Haines. Even vindictive Fred Galt. Men who had nothing to gain, small men who lacked the courage it took to stand against the current that Hank Dunning had started.

"Kim." Bonham brought his mouth close to Kim's ear. "You're getting out of here right after dark. You be ready. One minute either way might decide it. Don't waste no time."

"I don't want you . . ."

"Don't make no difference whether you want it or not. I owe you the same kind of a debt that Yuma owed me. It's the rest of 'em I'm worried about. I'd do it myself, but I need help to pull it off."

Turning, Bonham started across the room. Lane said, "Brit." Bonham made a slow turn to face him. Casually the sheriff opened a desk drawer and laid Kim's gun on the spur-scarred desk. "I made a jackass out of myself this morning just like Logan said. So did Galt and Luke Haines and everybody else who was in the line. We should have knowed the bank was good."

Bonham shifted his weight uncertainly. He said, "You're a little late thinking of that."

"I am for a fact." Lane laid a double-barreled shotgun on the desk beside Kim's Colt. "What I'm trying to say is that I know you're an honest man. You've done a hell of a lot for the country. Believed in it and stayed here. Even bucked old Sam Cody when he was riding high and handsome. Well, now you're an old man who deserves to die in bed with his boots off."

"I aim to," Bonham said evenly.

Lane gnawed off a chew of tobacco and slipped the plug

back into his pocket. "Naw, you don't aim to do no such thing. That whispering with Logan didn't fool nobody. You're fixing to bust him out of here. Now I'd hate to do it like hell, but if you make a try, I'll drill you the same as I would any man."

Bonham threw his stooped shoulders back, trying to gain all the height that he could. He said with dignity, "You'd be doing your duty, Ed," and walked out.

The sheriff dropped into his swivel chair and cocked his legs on his desk, chewing steadily until the hall floor stopped squeaking under Bonham's feet. He said then, "I've been wondering, Logan. That dinero wasn't on you. What'd you do with it?"

"So that's it. I wondered what you was working up to."

Lane straightened and swung his feet to the floor. "I wasn't working up to nothing."

"But you'd make a deal, wouldn't you?"

"I don't savvy," Lane said, his face a mask of innocent guile.

"If I split the dinero you think I stole, you'd shoot wide if Brit tries to break me out of here. That it?"

Lane choked. He got up and spit into the brass spittoon at the end of his desk. "Damn it, I didn't make no such proposition . . ."

"Yuma Bill had ten thousand dollars in his money belt, Ed. How would you like to have five of that?"

Lane sat down, scratching his bald head. "I'm listening."

"Aw, go to hell," Kim said wearily, and dropped down on his bunk.

"You'll be there afore I will," Lane bawled. "You don't need to think I'm gonna get myself filled with lead to protect a killing son like you. They'll haul you out of here tonight and you'll be dancing on air."

"I ain't surprised," Kim said. "No sir, I ain't surprised. Dunning really bought himself a sheriff when he pinned the star on you."

Lane leaned back in his chair. He said with smug satisfaction, "I got the star, ain't I? That's more'n you're getting from Clawhammer."

CHAPTER 11

ESCAPE

ED LANE had been in and out of his office all afternoon, apparently convinced that no effort would be made to break Kim out while it was daylight. Now, with darkness upon the town, he stayed at his desk, chewing steadily, eyes almost lidded shut, feet cocked in front of him.

Lying on his bunk, Kim watched the man, lamplight throwing a yellow glare on his shiny head. Kim wanted a cigarette, but his pride would not allow him to ask Lane for the makings.

It seemed very quiet. Kim climbed up on the bunk and looked through the window. The sky was clear now; stars glittered with cold brilliance. The sound of thunder had died, but lightning still played along the eastern horizon above the Continental Divide.

He sat down on his bunk again, impatience winding his nerves tight. Usually a lynch mob gave out its own peculiar sound. Some of the men would be drunk on Dunning's free whiskey. Others, probably Dunning and Fred Galt, would be cold sober. They would be the brains of the mob. There would be no fight, Ed Lane being the man he was. Still, they must think of some device which would make it appear that Lane had no responsibility for what was to happen.

Bonham would not be intimidated by what Lane had said. He and whoever was with him, Doc Frazee and Charlie Bemis perhaps, would make some kind of a try, but it was a question in Kim's mind which group would reach the jail first. If it came to a fight between them, Bonham was licked. Numbers favored the mob, and some of its members would be HD hands, better fighting men than the few townsmen who would be siding Bonham.

A noise behind the courthouse startled Kim. Horse? He might be imagining it. He rose, yawned and stretched, and stepped up on the cot again. There were three dark blobs out there that might be horses, but he couldn't be sure. At such a time a man's senses are not to be fully trusted, and the starlight was so thin that he might be seeing what he wanted to see and not what was actually out there.

Kim stepped down, saying casually, "Storm blew over."

"The big one ain't." Lane rose. "Too bad about Bonham.

72

Like I said, he's a fine old gent." He picked up the shotgun and sighted down the barrel. "Buckshot sure messes a man up. And don't count on Bonham doing the job. One of Dunning's boys is outside. I ain't playing this alone."

Hot words were on Kim's tongue. He wanted to say that if anything happened to Brit Bonham, Ed Lane would get his, too. But there was no use. Not unless Kim could get out of here with a gun in his hand. Whatever he said now would be an idle threat. He stood with his hands clenching the bars, hating Ed Lane as he had never hated a man before in his life.

The floor boards in the hall squealed. Lane grinned and picked up the shotgun. "Shut your eyes, Logan. This ain't gonna be purty."

Quick steps sounded closer, more boards squealed. Then Kim's eyes widened as surprise shocked him. It was Della Naylor who came in, not Brit Bonham. Lane was even more surprised than Kim. He stood staring at the girl uncertainly, his lips parted. Then he laid the shotgun down and scratched his head.

"You gave me a turn, Della," Lane said. "I figured you was old man Bonham aiming to bust this killing son loose."

Della shook her head. "I'm not Bonham." She wrinkled her pug nose. "Or do I look like him?"

"Hell no." Lane walked around the desk to her. "You're mighty purty, and you can't say that for that old goat."

She laughed. Kim had always liked the sound of her laugh, but now it struck him that there was a false note to it. He demanded, "Why ain't you home with Johnny?"

She looked past Lane at Kim, frowning. "That's a smart question. I'll tell you. First place Johnny isn't home. Second place, I've got an apology to make to Ed."

"Apology?" Lane reached out and patted her hands. "You don't need to make no apology to Ed Lane, not for nothing."

"Get out of here, Della," Kim shouted.

"Well, you'd do well to keep your mouth shut," Della said. "Ed's the kind who appreciates a girl, which is more than I can say about Johnny. Or you, either."

Lane laughed easily. "That's sure true. Leastwise I appreciate you."

"Where's Rocky?" Kim demanded.

"Gone home." Della drew away from Lane and danced across the floor to Kim's cell, her slim back to Lane, hips swaying. "Johnny's in the Belle Union getting drunk. Both cats are away, Ed. No reason the mouse shouldn't play."

"I wouldn't mind playing mouse," Lane said.

Della danced back toward the door, heels making clicking sounds on the floor. "About that apology, Ed. If I'd known

Kim had killed that poor old man, I'd never have made Johnny back up on his story. Rocky likes Kim. I just did it because she asked me to."

"Rocky's mistook, too," Lane said. "He's not worth much, Logan ain't."

Della stood in the doorway, scowling at Kim. Then she shrugged. "Well, he'll get what he's got coming. Rocky's the only one who'll be sorry." She started to turn, saying over her shoulder. "You going to be here all night, Ed?"

"I don't figure on it."

Lane took a step toward her, but she moved back into the dark hall, as elusive as a shadow. "Now Ed," she said. "What are you up to?"

"What are you up to coming here?" he demanded.

"To tell you I made a mistake about Kim." She laughed lightly. "And that Johnny isn't home, but that doesn't mean anything to you."

"How do I know you ain't hoorawing me?"

This time Della stood motionless while Lane came up to her. He put his arms around her, the lamplight falling past them, their single shadow darkening the middle of the yellow patch. Della offered her lips, whispering, "I wouldn't fool you, Ed."

Lane kissed her greedily, his attention so closely fixed that he was not aware of Rocky's presence. She slipped out of a dark corner behind him and hit him with the barrel of her gun, an upsweeping blow that brought him to his knees. He had stood too tall for her to do more. He tried to call out, but only a groaning muffled sound came out of him. Rocky jammed a wadded-up bandanna into his mouth and swung the gun again. He went limp and Rocky stepped away and let him fall.

"Good job," Della said, running into Lane's office. "How do you like my acting, Kim?"

"Too good. I wish you hadn't got into this."

Della grabbed Lane's keys from his desk and tried one in the lock of Kim's cell. It failed. A second failed, but the third turned the lock and Della pulled the door open. Rocky had come in and stood watching, trembling under the nervous pressure of the moment.

"Let's lock him up," Della said. "It won't help Ed's reputation any if they find him locked up in your cell. I hope they hang him."

Kim dragged Lane's limp body into the cell and locked the door, wondering how badly he was hurt. Blood trickled in a small scarlet stream across his bald head. He wheeled to the desk, scooped up his gun, and slid it into holster.

"Horses are in back," Rocky said, jerking her head toward

the front door. "Here." She pressed a sack of Durham and a package of cigarette papers into his hand. "I thought you'd be smoking all afternoon."

Kim said, "Thanks," and blew out the lamp, bringing total blackness to the room.

Della was halfway down the hall. Rocky gripped Kim's arm. She said, "The front door is propped open, but we can't just make a run for it. Pete Delaney's outside. He knows we're in here, so we've got to take care of him."

"Can't shoot him," Kim said. "Bring the whole wolf pack."

"Maybe we can work it like we did on Lane. You stay in the hall. Della's going to fetch Delaney in if she can."

They moved toward the front door, the floor boards squeaking. The hall was a dark tunnel, but apparently Della had reached the steps. She called, "Pete."

"Here." A man drifted up out of the darkness. "Anything wrong?"

"Plenty. Come here and look."

Rocky and Kim were at the end of the hall, the faint light from the street falling through the open doorway. Kim moved close to the wall and remained inside, but Rocky went on to stand beside Della.

"Hurry, Pete," Rocky said with quiet urgency. "The light's out."

The HD man swore. "You don't reckon Bonham got Logan out?"

"It's as black as a tomb in there," Rocky breathed. "We couldn't see. Maybe somebody shot Kim."

"No such luck as that," Delaney growled, and started up the steps. He reached the top one and stopped, suddenly suspicious. "What kind of a trick are you two pulling off? Ed had a light back there a minute ago."

"He hasn't now," Rocky said. "Have you got any matches?"

Rocky and Della were both on the top step, Delaney between them. For a moment he stood motionless, turning his head to look at one and then the other, the only sound that of his breathing.

"Yeah, I've got a match," Delaney said finally, "but I ain't going in there. Maybe you're sweet on Logan, Rocky. Maybe you got him out and when I go in there, he'll burn me down."

"I just want to see him get a square deal," Rocky flared. "I want to know what happened."

"I guess you're afraid of the dark," Della said scornfully. "Give me a match and I'll find out what's wrong."

"I ain't afraid of the dark," Delaney said, "but I'm afraid of Kim Logan, and I ain't the only one. I'm gonna get Dunning."

Delaney swung around to go back down the steps, but before he'd made the full turn, the girls grabbed his arms, Rocky calling, "Kim."

Delaney bawled a surprised oath, and perked his hands free, slamming both girls back against the courthouse wall, but it was something he had not expected, and it took a moment. Before he could lift his gun, Kim was on him.

Kim got his left arm around Delaney's neck and squeezed while he drove his right into the HD man's face. Delaney gurgled and tried to break free, but his frantic threshing accomplished nothing. His back was against Kim's stomach, and the best he could do was to lash backwards with a foot, his heel catching Kim on the shin and sending pain lancing up his leg.

"Bust him," Della urged. "Somebody's coming."

Given time, Kim could have choked him unconscious, but there was no time. Once the alarm was sounded, a dozen men would rush out of the Belle Union and Rocky and Della might get hurt. This was the sort of situation Brit Bonham had foreseen when he had warned Kim to be ready and not to waste time.

Kim pulled Delaney back into the hall, his left arm still hard against the man's throat, then he let go. Delaney, with nothing to support him, went down, his head rapping against the floor. He lay on his back, half-stunned. Kim dropped on him, knees slamming into the man's hard-muscled belly and driving breath out of him. He swung his right fist to Delaney's jaw. When he rose, Delaney lay still.

Wheeling, Kim plunged through the doorway. Rocky and Della were on the ground at the base of the steps, Rocky saying softly, "This way, Kim."

He glimpsed their shadowy figures as they faded toward the corner of the building. A man turning in from the street heard their pounding steps. He yelled, "Dunning," and fired, a wild high shot. Kim ran after the girls, hit a slick spot still wet from the afternoon rain, and fell headlong. He scrambled up as the man threw another shot that went wide, and sprinted on to the rear of the courthouse as Della swung into saddle.

"I'm going home, Kim," Della called. "Don't get into a fight with 'em. I don't want Johnny hurt." Swinging her horse, she rode away.

"Here." Bonham pressed the reins into Kim's hands. "Rocky's black. Do what she says. She's got it all planned."

Rocky was in the saddle now, calling in a hurry-up tone, "Come on, come on."

Kim stepped up, not liking it. "What'd you get the girls into this for, Brit?"

"Rocky's idea, not mine," Bonham said, and drifted away into the darkness.

Rocky was already riding into the cluster of deserted cabins that lay back of the courthouse, holding her horse down, hoofs dropping into the soft earth with faint sucking sounds. The hoof beats of Della's running horse came clearly to Kim. She was heading east toward the mesa.

Kim reined in beside Rocky, saying angrily, "I can't let her go alone. They're likely to kill her before they find out who she is."

"Don't be a fool," Rocky said sharply. "She's got the fastest horse in the valley and I think she's the best rider. They'll never catch her. Or if they did, all she'd have to do would be to holler. Johnny'll be with the posse."

Rocky turned into an old shed and dismounted. For a moment Kim sat his saddle, fighting his stubborn pride. Then he stepped down and stood beside Rocky, knowing the girl was right. Della was a good rider. He had often met her crossing the valley to her folk's ranch, or on narrow mountain trails. If he followed, there would be a fight, and the posse would have men in it Kim did not want to kill.

A great clatter had broken out in front of the courthouse. Men shouted; there was some wild shooting. Then Dunning's great voice, "We're losing time. I'll take charge here." A moment later they swept out of town to the east, eight or ten of them, but already Della's hoofbeats had faded. In this vast blanket of darkness there would be little chance of finding her.

Kim gripped Rocky's arm and turned her to face him, but he saw only a pale oval that seemed to be devoid of expression. He asked, "Why did you and Della do this?"

"We've got a fight on our hands," she said. "When you get Peg figured out, you'll lead us. We couldn't let them hang a man we needed."

"I don't think Dutch Heinz meant . . ."

"Oh yes he did. We're not going to run again. Maybe you don't know it, but Dad and Della's father and most of our neighbors were driven out of the valley by Sam Cody. We won't be driven again, Kim. Not by Peg or Dunning or anybody."

He had never heard the whole story of Sam Cody's coming to the valley. He had never asked who had suffered from Cody's pushing tactics because he had not considered it his business. Naturally Peg had not volunteered much information about it. Now he understood Shorty Avis's hatred for everything that belonged to Clawhammer. Avis had classed him with Heinz.

"We'd better ride," Kim said.

For a moment Rocky did not move. Her face still lifted to his as if her eyes were trying to pierce the darkness. She said, "I was pretty young when it happened, so I don't remember much about the trouble, but I've heard Dad say that if they had fought together, they could have licked Cody. It'll be the same again unless somebody can make us work together."

It was the old, time-proved technique of divide and conquer. Kim had seen it used many times. A single large outfit could clear a range of the small spreads by taking them one at a time, but if they had united, the small spreads would have been stronger than their common enemy. To weld a bunch of small cowmen together was always a problem. Kim, knowing the mesa ranchers, doubted that it could be done.

"I'm beholden to you," Kim said at last, "and if it comes to a fight, I'm your man. I don't think it will. Peg's got all she can do to hold Dunning off without bothering you folks."

Turning, Rocky stepped into the saddle. She waited until Kim had swung up. Then she said, "It would be an accident if we ran into them tonight. By sunup we'll be hid out."

"I'm not going to dodge around like a rabbit," Kim said hotly.

"Then go back and sit in jail. If you want your neck stretched, they'll accommodate you."

"All right," he said.

They threaded their way through the cabins until they reached open country, then swung toward the stage road that crossed the valley. Reaching it, they turned directly east until they came to the side road that led to Clawhammer. Kim reined up, saying, "You go on home and stay out of trouble."

"Where are you going?"

"Clawhammer."

"You don't think you'll get the man who killed Yuma Bill out there, do you?"

"I might."

"Or maybe you think Peg will hide you out."

"I've got to have grub. Only thing to do is to duck the posse till I get my hands on Phil Martin. When I do, he'll sing another tune about what he saw."

She took a ragged breath, her saddle squeaking as she shifted her weight. "Kim, you think we hate Clawhammer so much that we're judging Peg wrong. That it?"

"That's about it. Peg's into trouble up to her neck. Looks like your bunch and Clawhammer had better throw in together, or Dunning will have the valley."

"I've never told you what I know about Peg because you wouldn't believe me. You'd just say I hated her. I do, but hating her doesn't make me blind. You are."

"I don't go switching around when I take a job," he said

78

hotly. "Sure Peg's greedy just like you say, but that ain't a crime."

"I'll ride along with you," she said. "If you find out she doesn't want anything to do with you now, will you go with me?"

"Sure, but what'll you do if you're guessing wrong on Peg?"

"I'm not," she said.

Rocky turned off the stage road, following the twin ruts that led to Clawhammer. Kim caught up with her, admitting to himself that she might be right about his being blind. It had always been a fault with him, believing in people he wanted to believe in until the evidence was final. Loyalty, he knew, could be a fault as well as a virtue. Peg's faith in Dutch Heinz proved that.

There was a pattern of evil that lay upon the valley, a shadow as dark as this night, evil that had brought about the death of Yuma Bill and had very nearly put a rope on Kim's neck. The trouble was that both evil and good were often disguised as one another.

Now, with the cool night wind on his face and the tension of the long afternoon finally lifted, he had time to think about Yuma Bill's death. Dutch Heinz could have been the killer. Peg could have told him that Yuma Bill would be at Smith's cabin. That thought brought him squarely back to Peg. It was what Rocky would have him believe, but he could not.

CHAPTER 12

HALF TRUTH

IT WAS near midnight when Kim and Rocky forded Ganado Creek, water lancing out from their horses' hoofs like curving arrows, faintly silvered by the starlight. The big ranch house sprawled before them, the barn and corrals to their left. The place seemed very quiet; there was no light anywhere around it.

"You can't stay here long, Kim," Rocky said. "When they don't pick up your trail, they'll come here."

"I reckon," Kim agreed.

The dog charged around the corner of the house, barking fiercely. Kim reined up, calling, "Shut up, Nero." He swung down, looping his reins over the hitch pole. The dog jumped around, whining eagerly, and Kim stooped to pet him.

Kim waited a moment, expecting a light to come to life

inside the house, but there was none. Then old Limpy called out from the darkness, "Who is it?"

"Kim."

"Who's with you?"

"Rocky Avis."

There was a moment of silence. Limpy, Kim was sure, would doubt the girl's presence. Then the old man drifted up, thumbing a match to flame when he was close to Rocky. The tiny light spluttered, briefly showing the girl's small chin and sharp nose and dark eyes filled with cool defiance. Then the match flickered out.

"Didn't believe it, did you, Limpy?" Rocky asked.

"No, I sure didn't," the old man admitted. "What'n hell you doing here?"

"Making company for Kim."

"Maybe I'd better ask what you're doing here, Kim. Thought you was in the calaboose for beefing that hombre you took off the stage."

"Kicked a couple bars loose. Sure didn't get no help from Clawhammer."

"Didn't have no help to give you," Limpy snapped. "If you had some powder to burn, why didn't you burn it on one of Dunning's toughs?"

"You making out I drilled Yuma?"

"Lane had an eyewitness, the way we heard it."

"Phil Martin," Kim said hotly. "You believe him?"

"Maybe," the old man said. "Maybe not. All I know is we don't want a hunted man hiding out on Clawhammer."

"You see," Rocky said quietly. "He's been told what to say."

Kim wheeled and started toward the house. Limpy called, "Come back here. Peg's been asleep for a couple of hours."

"She'll wake up," Kim said, and went on.

"Damn it," Limpy bawled. "You come back here. I've got a Winchester . . ."

"But you won't use it," Rocky said. "I've got a gun, too."

Limpy muttered something and subsided. Kim went into the house and striking a match, lit a lamp. Then he crossed the room to Peg's door and tapped. There was no response. He tapped again, louder. Another moment of silence, then Peg called sleepily, "Who is it?"

"Kim. I've got to talk to you."

"Just a minute. Wait till I get my robe on."

He moved back to the table and stood there, worriedly tapping his fingers on the oak surface. Now that the moment was here, he wondered what he would say. He wouldn't tell her he was riding out of the valley to duck a murder charge. Besides, she still needed him.

He heard her door open and looked up. She was wearing a dark blue robe, the cord tightly tied around her small waist, her hair falling far down her back in a red mass. She came to him with quick eagerness, her hands out. She reached him and put her arms around him, and she clung to him for a moment. Then she tipped her head back, eyes anxiously searching his face.

"I've been worried about you, Kim. Bonham sent word you were in jail. How did you get out?"

Rocky was wrong about her. That was the first thought which came to him, and he felt the tension leave him. Perhaps, as Rocky said, he was blind to Peg Cody's faults, but regardless of those faults, she had been anxious about him. A man was a fool for trusting a woman only when that woman was not loyal.

He said, "I'm out. That's what counts. I've been doing some worrying myself. You still haven't got anybody here but Limpy. Nothing to keep Dunning from riding in and wiping you out."

"He won't," she said with some impatience. "I keep telling you that. You're the one who's in trouble."

"I won't be soon as I get the truth out of Martin. He's the one who tried to put the rope on my neck. Another one of Dunning's tricks to get at Clawhammer, I reckon."

She stepped back and shook her head. "You won't be any help to Clawhammer if they get the rope on your neck, Kim. You've got to get out of the valley and stay out."

He frowned, eyes searching her face. He could not keep the doubt from nagging his mind. It was a poor kind of loyalty that didn't work two ways.

"I'm not getting out yet," he said roughly. "I've got to buy some time, Peg. That's all I need."

"I can't help you, Kim." She shook her head. "I shouldn't have said that because I know you didn't expect it. You wouldn't want to pull me into trouble with the law."

When he had come here, he had had no intention of staying. More than anything else, he wanted to prove Rocky wrong. Now he said, "You could hide me out."

"Not when you're an outlaw, Kim. I'd like to help you, but the best thing for both of us is for you to put a lot of miles between you and Ganado."

He was still looking at her, trying to see something on her face that wasn't there. Her eyes seemed to hold concern for him, but he could not tell what was behind them. Women, he thought, were natural born actors. Della Naylor had fooled Ed Lane, and he had a hunch that Peg was fooling him now as effectively as Della had fooled Lane.

He took a deep breath, remembering his dreams he had never fully voiced to anyone. Clawhammer might have been all he had hoped for, his and Peg's, if he could have proved to her she needed him. Not in the way she needed Dutch Heinz, but in the way that one woman needs one particular man, prove it so that she would obey the desires of her heart instead of the logic of her mind.

He thought of Tonto Miles, of facing him in the morning sunlight. It had seemed to him they were the same, two men hired for their guns, yet there had been the hope that he was more to Peg Cody. Now he sensed that he had made the mistake of reaching for something he could never possess. He had found only the shadow, not the substance.

"You want me to run?" he demanded. "Let folks think I killed Yuma?"

"You've got to," she said. "Don't you see? Clawhammer can't protect a man who's wanted by the law."

"Looks like it ought to make some difference who the man is."

She shook her head. "Not when it concerns Clawhammer."

He made one quick step and took her into his arms. He kissed her, letting her know his feelings, trying to put everything into that kiss which he could not put into words. He failed. He realized it at once. There had been something in her last night; desire, a demand, a hunger for him. It was not in her now.

He let her go and stepped back to the table. "I didn't ask you to marry me last night because I wanted you to feel that I could do something for you. I mean, something bigger than just riding around and making a show of my gun and seeing that Dunning stayed on his side of the creek. I did it today. It was something you couldn't have bought for all the dollars in the valley."

"I know," she said coolly. "You saved the bank and Dunning didn't get my notes. But Lane arrested you for murder. That changes everything."

"For a murder I didn't do," he said hotly "That shouldn't change anything. You're the one who's changing things."

She shook her head. "It's like I said. I threw myself at you and you threw me back. You changed both our lives for us then." She made a quick gesture as if dismissing it forever. "It's a poor kind of woman who has no pride. I have mine, Kim."

"You threw Clawhammer at me, not yourself. Maybe some day you'll find you're a woman, not a ranch." He turned toward the door and swung back before he reached it. "Yuma Bill didn't sleep any last night. He said he heard you ride out before dawn."

82

Her lips made a tight line; wariness crept Into her eyes. "He dreamed it."

"I don't think so. I'm pretty good at forgetting things I don't want to remember, but there's one thing I can't forget. You had the idea for Yuma to stay at Smith's cabin while I rode into town. He was killed at the cabin."

"Go on," she breathed. "Say the rest of it."

"I don't need to say it. Heinz wanted to kill Yuma last night for the dinero that was in the shoe box."

"And I said no. Remember?"

"Yeah, I remember. But after that you had time to think it over."

"Go on, Kim. Say it. Say that I killed Yuma Bill."

He stood looking at her, not more than a step away, nagged by a suspicion that had been buried in his mind all through the afternoon. Still, even after all of this, he could not put it in words. "I'll be riding," he said, and turned toward the door.

"Kim." She gripped his arm and turned him to face her. "You know now that the only thing I really love is Clawhammer."

He nodded. "I guess that's plain enough. You're making a mistake, Peg. You'll come out holding the short end of the stick."

"I'll take my chances . . ."

From outside Rocky called, "Kim, they're coming."

Startled, Peg asked, "Who's that?"

"Rocky Avis."

"You mean . . ." Peg shook her head and began to laugh. "Well, I've been a bigger fool than I ever thought I'd be. You've been in love with Shorty Avis's brat all the time. I asked you last night and you lied to me."

He saw anger in her that swiftly swelled to a wild fury. She would believe what she wanted to believe, no more and no less. He said, "Reckon I'm fired."

"You're fired all right. You bet you're fired. If you're smart, you'll keep riding till you're a thousand miles from here, and don't think you can stay and save your friends on the mesa. Clawhammer needs all the range on this side of the creek. All of it. Do you hear?" Her voice rose until it was the scream of an angry shrew. "I'm building an empire, but I don't need your help. Keep riding and take the Avis kid with you."

He had seen her talk to other men like this, but it was the first time she had ever whipped him with her tongue. Her eyes were bright with fury; her face was red and the corners of her mouth were working. There seemed to be no reason for it, then it occurred to him that she wanted no more responsibility for him; she wanted to feel that she owed him nothing.

Rocky called again, more urgently this time, "Kim, they're coming."

He said, "So long, Peg," and wheeling, left the house.

Limpy, still standing beside Rocky's horse, said, "You'd better travel, mister. I'll steer 'em the wrong way. Clawhammer owes you that much."

"Thanks, Limpy." Kim stepped up. "Look out for her, will you?"

"Sure, but there's only so much a man can do for her."

"So long," Kim said.

"This way," Rocky called.

The posse, quite close now, was coming in on the road that Kim and Rocky had followed a few minutes before. Rocky turned south. Kim swung in beside her, surprised, for he had supposed she would want to go home. To do that, she would have had to cross the creek and swing west. Instead she followed the bench that rose to the left, an indistinct wall in the darkness.

They rode slowly, their horses' hoofs making little sound in the soft grass carpet. The racket of the incoming posse died; then Dunning called out in his great voice, "We're looking for Kim Logan. Seen him?"

Kim could not hear what Limpy said. He wondered what Peg would say. When he had left her, she had been furious enough to want to see him lynched. He doubted whether her anger had cooled so that she would cover up for him. They went on, Kim listening. He had expected pursuit, but there was none. Either Peg had lied for him, or Limpy had sent the posse across the creek on a wild goose chase that might take hours before they found that their man had gone the other way.

The lights in the ranch house flowed together and made a tiny pinpoint, then it was lost to sight. Presently Rocky said, "There's a trail here. We'll swing up on the mesa."

They were two, perhaps three miles south of the creek. Kim said, "I don't savvy this. You're putting the canyon between us and your place."

"That's exactly what I aim to do. We're not going to my place. Limpy will tell them who was with you, so they'll hightail up there."

Kim laughed. "Shorty'll sure be surprised."

"He'll be mighty mad," she said worriedly. "I don't know what he'll do."

"He won't like you sashaying around through the hills with me."

"I know he won't. If I ever go home, he'll rawhide me, and maybe get out his shotgun and make you marry me."

"He wouldn't need his shotgun for that."

She didn't say anything then. They climbed to the sage flat above the bench and angled southeast. This was open country, dotted by runty cedars. A slim moon was showing above the peaks to the east; the stars still glittered in cold brilliance from a clear, wind-swept sky.

Rocky reined up and untying her coat from behind her saddle, slipped into it. She said, her voice expressionless, "You know, Kim, I wouldn't care for a marriage that needed a shotgun."

"It wouldn't . . ."

"No, don't say that. You've had Peg in your mind for a long time. I don't know whether you ever really loved her or not. Maybe you were in love with Clawhammer. Either way, it'll take some time to get it out of your system."

He rolled a smoke and lighted it, the flame throwing a brief light upon his wide mouth and square chin. The match flickered out; he broke it between thumb and forefinger, destroying the last spark before he threw it into the grass. He said, "You've got some pretty sorry notions about me, Rocky. I can't figure out why you've gone to so much trouble for me lately."

"Not sorry notions, Kim. It's just that you're two men."

"Never knew I was twins," he jeered.

"I do. I've known it for a long time. There's the man you have been and the man you could be. I keep wondering which one you're finally going to be."

"Makes me quite a mess, don't it?"

"It'll be a mess if you ride out of the country now," she said. "Some day men like you will disappear, but that day hasn't come yet. Maybe it's a good thing. We need you."

"You think the country will be better off if men like me disappear?"

"Yes. I mean, the man you have been. Anyhow, I couldn't blame you if you did ride on."

"I couldn't," he said quietly. "There's plenty here to hold me."

"You mean you wouldn't leave a murder charge?"

"That's part of it."

"What's the rest of it?"

"You ain't ready to hear about it."

"I'm ready to listen when you're ready to tell it."

"Maybe I won't have to tell it."

"You always have to tell a woman," she said.

They went on, directly east now, the flat gradually lifting toward the rim that lay in front of them. Presently they were in the timber, limbs interlacing above them and blotting the starlight. Rocky rode ahead, following the twisting narrow trail in a way that brought increasing admiration for her in Kim's mind.

They stopped at a spring to water their horses, the first gray hint of dawn touching the eastern sky. Rocky said, "Almost there."

"You're riding through this country like you know it."

"I do. I like to ride at night. Pa claims I'm half owl."

They took the trail again, climbing steep pitches, crossing small parks and coming into the timber again, hoofs dropping silently into the thick mat of pine needles that was seldom disturbed except by the swift passage of a deer. They splashed across a small stream and Rocky turned to follow it.

Daylight had moved in around them, but the air was still sharp with the night chill. Another five minutes brought them to a cabin at the lower end of a long stretch of aspens that made a splash of light green against the darker mass of the pines.

"This is it," Rocky said, and swung down.

She stood there for a moment, one hand holding to the saddle horn, bone-weary. Kim stepped down and came to her, saying, "We should have stopped. You're all in."

"Not quite." She gave him a quick smile that was a light on her face. "They'll never find us here. We can sleep for a week."

"Us? Look here, Rocky, I'm not going to let 'em find you with me. You . . ."

"You'll have a hard time getting rid of me." She motioned to a shed behind the cabin. "Put the horses up. I'll get breakfast." She yawned and rubbed her eyes. "You know, Kim, I don't think a week will be long enough. A month sounds more like it."

She had not brought any food. He wondered what she would find to cook breakfast with, but when he had finished with the horses and went in, aspen chunks were burning in the stove with bright crackling pops, and the cabin was filled with the fragrance of boiling coffee and frying bacon.

"How did you . . ."

She turned from the stove, brushing at a stray strand of black hair that fell across her forehead. "Magic. I said hocus-pocus. Then I waved my hands and said abracadabra. That was all it took."

"I didn't know you were that smart."

He looked around, his amazement growing. The timber around Pass Creek Valley was full of prospectors' cabins, but none that Kim had seen were like this. It was clean and tight with a bunk at one end, the stove at the other, and a small pine table and two benches in the middle. Shelves be-hind the stove were filled with cans of food.

Rocky motioned to a bucket on the packed dirt floor. "Fetch in some more water, will you, Kim."

When he returned, she had poured the coffee. She said, "This isn't much of a breakfast, but it'll do." She yawned again. "I'm about to fall over in my tracks. I didn't get much sleep the night before, either. By the time I took the body in . . ."

"Body? You mean you took that hombre in who fell off the cliff?"

She laughed shakily. "My head's kind of fuzzy. I wasn't going to tell you that. I just didn't have time to go home and get Pa. Besides, I wanted to be in town when you and Yuma Bill got there." She dropped down on one of the benches, suddenly defiant. "I wasn't sure Pa would do it. He's awful stubborn sometimes."

He stood looking down at her, more humble than he had ever been before in his life. He had always thought of her as more girl than woman, probably because she was small-bod-ied, or perhaps because she seemed child-like in so many of her desires. Now he realized that what he had considered childishness was not that at all. She was a product of the life she lived: simple, without pretense or sham, almost brutally honest with herself and others, and filled with a kind of courage that few men could claim.

"If I live a million years," he said, "I'll never be able to pay you . . ."

"Sit down," she broke in sharply. "You don't owe me any-thing, so don't talk that way. The trouble with you is that you've always thought there was nothing you and your gun couldn't do. You're going to find out different."

"I have already," he said, and took the bench across the table from her.

CHAPTER 13

PROMISE OF EVIDENCE

IT WAS late afternoon when Kim woke. He had gone to sleep in the shadow of the shed. Now the sun had moved far to the west and was drenching him with its warmth. He got up, and walking to the creek, washed his face. He had a brief glimpse of himself in the unruffled surface of a deep pool and shook his head in disapproval. He needed a shave, his yellow hair was matted and overlong, and his gaunt face seemed more gaunt than ever.

"You look pretty damn tough, fella," he said aloud.

He hunkered beside the stream in the shade of a pine and rolled a smoke. Constant riding had honed his long body down to skin and hard muscle and bone; never-ending vigilance had cut lines around his eyes that made him look years older than he was. Now, and it seemed as if it was the first time in months, he felt no need for vigilance. He was at peace. The impending violence which had long threatened the valley would still be like a stream running in full flood, but at this moment it seemed so remote that it could be shoved into the outer fringe of thought.

A jay flew by, a flash of vivid blue. Overhead a woodpecker was working on a tree with jack-hammer violence. Below him a foot-long trout flashed across the pool like a black knifing shadow. It struck Kim then that he had been too busy trying to keep alive in a world of trouble to notice things like this. This was another world, Rocky's world. She had shared its strength and honesty; it had made her what she was.

It was strange, he thought, how he had lived in country like this most of his life, yet actually he had not known it at all. He had merely passed through it. He flipped his cigarette stub into the creek and lay back, staring at the clean sky.

There was no wind, just the quiet steady downpouring of the sun's rays. Here were the smells of a moist earth and pine needles and wild flowers, all flowing together into one common mountain smell. Here were sounds, the squawking of the jay, the rhythmical clattering of the woodpecker, the creek song as it dropped over a rock ledge above the pool, sounds that fell together as naturally as those from a trained orchestra, and paradoxically, did not mar the great silence.

He did not know that Rocky had come up behind him until she asked, "Sleeping?"

He jumped and rolled and grabbed for his gun, the natural reaction of a man who has long lived with danger. Then he lay motionless, staring up at her and feeling foolish. He started to tell her to never sneak up on him like that again, but he caught himself in time. She hadn't sneaked up on him. It was her natural way of moving.

"No. Dreaming, I guess. How'd you sleep?"

"I didn't. I just died."

He sat up, feeling of his stubbly chin. "I took a look at myself while ago. Sure handsome."

"You look natural." She dropped down beside him. "I didn't tell you this morning, but I think Brit will be along, so I might as well. This is his cabin."

He reached for the makings. "Comes out to fish, I suppose."

"No. He thinks this is still mining country. He's got a prospect hole across the creek." She motioned toward it. "Over behind that brush. He tells folks in town that he comes up here to fish, but it's really to dig."

"How did you know about his cabin?"

"I stumbled onto it during a storm. Brit was here. He swore me to secrecy. Made me promise that I'd make all my children be hard-rock miners if I ever told anybody, but that promise won't apply to you. He knew I was bringing you out here."

"Sure be awful, having your children turn out to be hard-rock miners."

She laughed. "It would for a fact. I like it on top of the ground."

"So that's why there was grub."

She nodded. "He keeps enough here to last two or three weeks. He was snowed in once."

"Funny a banker would get the notion he was a prospector."

"Not so funny. Doc Frazee's the same way. They'd like to see Ganado come back and the only way they know to bring it back is to have another mining boom." She lay on the bank, her slim body curled so that the hem of her riding skirt worked up to her knees. She didn't notice; her eyes were on the pool, her tanned face eagerly alert. "Kim, there's enough trout down there for supper. Want me to get Brit's pole for you?"

"I wouldn't know what to do with a fish if he reached up and hollered for me to pull him out."

She rolled over, tugging at her skirt. "You mean you've never gone fishing?"

"Not since I was a kid. Been too busy."

For no reason that Kim could see, she was suddenly angry. "Too busy! Hell's bells, if all you've done was to ride around stomping snakes, you'd better start fishing."

He had smoked his cigarette down and thrown the stub into the creek. Automatically he reached for paper and tobacco and rolled another, sensing the same scorn that had been in her when he had stopped with Yuma Bill and she had talked about him being a snake stomper. He said nothing until he lighted his cigarette. She was sitting up, sharp little chin resting on her knees, dark eyes staring morosely at the big pine across the creek.

"Ever figure you might have me wrong?" he said.

"No. I don't, either. There's a place for fighting and a

89

place for work, but you don't know anything about the work. Just the fighting."

He grinned, the cigarette dangling from one corner of his mouth, the blue smoke curling up lazily before his lean face. "Maybe I'm a better snake stomper than a brush popper, but I've done a little staring at the rear of a cow, too. I helped drive a Texas herd plumb to Dakota. Surprised?"

"I sure am," she said skeptically. "I didn't think you'd ever take a chance on ruining your gun hand with a rope or a branding iron."

"Here's another surprise. I've got a thousand dollars in Bonham's bank. Saved it since I got here. Had a notion I'd like to own a little outfit. Up by your place, maybe. Anyhow, I thought I'd keep on working for Peg as long as I could so I'd have a stake when I started."

"You might try poker," she jeered.

"Naw, I'm about as bad a player as Johnny Naylor. That's why I was broke when I got here." He tossed a rock into the creek and watched the ripples spread across the pool. "Just before I left Yuma Bill yesterday morning, he said something about throwing in with me and buying a ranch here in the valley."

She stared at him for a long moment, lips parted as she thought about what he had said. "When he was murdered, you lost your chance."

"Any chance except what I make myself. A man don't buy many cows and calves with a thousand dollars."

"Well, I am surprised," Rocky said. "It's the other side of you I was talking about."

He grinned wryly. "I've done some thinking but not much talking. I did a lot more thinking after I met Yuma Bill. Seems like I can't forget the hombre who fell off the rim. And Tonto Miles. Sooner or later I'll get the same." He threw his cigarette away in a sudden violent gesture. "A man can't help dying alone, but it's sure hell to live alone."

"I know," she breathed. "I know." She stiffened and was silent, head cocked. Then she said, "Somebody's coming up the trail. Must be Brit. I'll get supper. You cut some wood."

She jumped up and ran into the cabin. Kim sat motionless for a moment, listening, but he heard nothing. He got up, shaking his head. Compared to most of the men he had ridden with, his ears were good, but Rocky made him feel like a greenhorn.

There was a pile of dry aspen in one corner of the shed; an ax leaned against the log wall. He began to chop, watching the trail below the cabin, and presently Brit Bonham appeared. Kim carried an armload of wood into the cabin and when he came out, Bonham had dismounted in front.

"Well, I see you outran 'em," Bonham said. "Figured you would. Don't reckon nobody in the country knows these hills like Rocky does unless it's Della."

Kim told him what had happened, and asked, "Dunning get back to town?"

Bonham shook his head. "Hadn't got back when I left. Kind o' worries me. Dunning sure don't like failures, and so far that's all he's had. Can't do no damage, though, I guess."

"He can play hell with Clawhammer."

Bonham's brows lifted. "Thought you said Peg fired you."

"She did, but I still don't cotton to the notion of Dunning moving across the creek."

"Well, Peg's old Sam Cody's daughter, and I reckon he taught her how to take care of herself. Catch any fish?"

"No."

"Then you've been wasting your day. Take care of my mare. I'll catch our supper."

By the time Kim had finished staking out the mare and cut another armload of wood, Bonham had pulled three pan-sized trout out of the pool. He cleaned and brought them in, saying, "Can't understand a man not fishing when he's got a chance. Good for your soul, Kim."

Rocky looked up from setting the table. "He's never had time to learn, Brit."

"Time," Bonham snorted. "Say, when a man hasn't got time to learn to fish, he's almighty busy. Want me to fry 'em, Rocky?"

"Go ahead," she said.

It was a silent meal, a sudden impatience in Kim at this inactivity. Finishing his coffee, he rose and walked to the door. The sun was down now, and the timber had blotted up most of the thinning light. Rocky had lighted a lamp, and Kim's shadow made a long dark splotch in the rectangle of lamplight spilling out through the doorway.

He rolled a smoke, thinking of what had to be done. He couldn't stay here, and as things stood now, he couldn't go back to Ganado. Still, if Phil Martin was in town, that was where Kim must go. Martin had placed the murder charge against him, so Martin was the one who could clear him.

Without turning, Kim asked, "Martin still in Ganado?"

"Yeah. Doc's keeping him. Seems like he should have gone to bed instead of sashaying around. Now he's a purty sick man."

"Brit, did you know that Yuma Bill was going into the cattle business here?" Rocky asked. "He was planning on taking Kim in as a partner."

"Well, I ain't surprised," Bonham said. "He sold out most of his holdings around Las Animas. I figured he'd stay hereabouts, and if he'd lived, he couldn't have kept his fingers off a ranch."

"What's going to happen to that money Kim brought to you?" Rocky asked.

"Well, that's something I've been asking myself," Bonham said somberly. "Yuma getting beefed sure put things into a mess. I doubt that he left a will, and he didn't have a single living relative. I know that."

"Then he'd want you to have it, you and Kim, wouldn't he?"

"I guess he would."

"Then why don't you use it to buy a big herd and let Kim have his ranch?"

Kim walked back to the table. "She's trying to make a working man out of me."

"It's what you want, isn't it?" Rocky demanded.

"I told you it was, but taking a dead man's money don't seem the right way to get it."

"Maybe marrying a redhead with a ranch would be?" Rocky flared.

"Maybe."

"It'd be right enough, Kim," Bonham said slowly. "As soon as I see the bank ain't gonna need it, I wouldn't be against doing something like that, only . . ."

He paused, turning his eyes from Rocky to Kim and back to the girl, his face thoughtful. Rocky asked, "Only what?"

"I ain't sure." Bonham got up and walked to the stove. He stood with his back to it, craggy face mirroring the uncertainty that gripped him. "I just ain't sure. You see, Rocky, me and Doc Frazee and Charlie Bemis, well, we're old. Our string's about wound up. The trouble is that the other bunch are young men. Johnny Naylor and Luke Haines and Fred Galt ain't what you'd call real solid."

"Say the rest of it, Brit," Kim said tonelessly. "I'm a fiddle-foot who's likely to be dragging out of here tomorrow."

"Well, damn it, you are," Bonham said, "and there ain't nobody else who can put the brake on Dunning. Or Peg, neither, if she gets some of old Sam's ideas."

"She's already got them. Brit, you're forgetting one thing." Rocky leaned forward. "My people."

Bonham gestured impatiently. "And you're forgetting that when Sam Cody made a few faces at 'em, they tucked their tails and lined out for the mesa, your dad included. Old Sam moved in. The east side of the valley is Clawhammer range whether you like it or not. Now that money is a kind of trust, you might say, and I've got to decide what to do with it along the line of what Yuma Bill would want."

"Like planting the right seed," Kim said.

Bonham gave him a defiant glance. "I don't know if you're trying to hooraw me or not, but that's exactly what I mean. He kind o' stole that money in the first place. Then he got a change of heart, but there wasn't no way to give it back, so he was bent on doing some good with it."

"Wouldn't it be good to bring peace to the valley?" Rocky asked.

Bonham shook his head. "You can't turn the clock back, Rocky, and I ain't sure that putting Kim on a ranch would stop Dunning or Peg."

"He's done pretty well so far," Rocky said.

"Just a skirmish. The big fight's still ahead, and I doubt that we've got enough on our side to win it."

"I'm going back to Ganado," Kim said, "and I'll get a different story out of Martin."

"Doc Frazee's working on Martin already." Bonham came back to the table. "Kim, where would you have gone if you'd been Salty Smith?"

"Wouldn't be north. No place to go. Wouldn't be west 'cause that'd take him past Dunning's spread. He'd have a rough trip getting across the line into New Mexico if he went south. So I reckon he'd head for the pass and go to Del Norte."

Pleased, Bonham laughed. "That's the way everybody but Smith would figure. Not old Salty, though. He'd ask himself what folks would expect him to do, then he'd cross 'em up. He headed south, but he didn't try getting across the line. He's in Sky City."

"He couldn't hide in a dinky burg like that. Dunning's sure to find him."

"That's what I figure. If he does, he'll shut Smith's mouth for good, but Smith thinks he's safe. Fatty York runs the hotel and he's a friend of Smith's."

"How do you know Salty's there?"

Bonham laughed again, proud of himself. "I kind o' tricked Fatty. Soon as the posse left Ganado I sent a man to Sky City. You see, Smith never kept much money on him. Drank it up as fast as his pension came in, so I talked him into putting ten dollars in the bank every month for burial money. Kind of proud, Smith is. He didn't want charity, so he's been depositing the ten dollars and drinking up the rest. Well, I sent a note to Fatty York along with a hundred dollars, telling him it was Smith's burial money but to use it to take care of him. York took it. That means Smith's there, or York wouldn't have touched it."

"I'd better go see Smith." Kim picked up his hat. "Dunning might make the same guess you did."

"Wouldn't surprise me if he had a man down there already," Bonham said. "I thought you'd want to see what you could do with Smith. If you're gonna get yourself cleared, it'll be Smith or Martin who does it."

Kim moved to the door, then turned back, smiling a little as he pinned his eyes on Rocky's grave face. "Thanks for everything, Shamrock."

She rose and walked to him, worried but not angry as she usually was when he called her by her name. She said in a low desperate voice, "You can't go, Kim. Not yet."

"I've got to. You helped me buy some time. That's what I needed."

"You haven't bought enough. You might as well have stayed in Ganado."

"No. We had a ride and some fun. I'm just sorry you had to risk your neck to save mine."

She tilted her head back so that she could see his face. She said, "Kim, I wanted to be with you long enough so you'd trust me and know I'm not lying to you."

"I've been with you that long," he said quickly.

She put her hands on his arms, gripping them tightly. "Then believe this. Peg and Dunning aren't fighting. She's in love with him."

There was nothing she could have said that would have shocked him more than that, and he let his face show it. He said, "You're mistaken. You must be."

"No. I know what I'm talking about. I've spied on them. I'm not ashamed of it, either. I wouldn't spy on anyone else, but I did them. Della has, too. There's a place up Ganado Canyon where they meet. We've seen him kiss her. I tell you they're working together."

"What do you think, Brit?" Kim asked.

"Hard to believe," the banker said, "but it explains some things I've wondered about. Dunning's done a lot of talking about busting Clawhammer, but he ain't done much busting."

"But what would it get them?"

"I couldn't say," Bonham said slowly. "On the face of it there don't seem to be much sense to talk about fighting while they're kissing each other on the side."

"You don't believe me, do you, Kim?" Rocky cried. "You think I'm lying because I hate Peg."

"I just think you're wrong."

'All right," she breathed. "Believe anything you want to, but don't go back to Clawhammer. Promise me you won't."

"I can't make a promise like that."

"Kim, you owe me your life," she whispered, her hands still clutching his arms, her knuckles white. "Kim, Kim, don't throw it away. If you go back to Clawhammer, you'll never get away alive."

"I'm beholden to you," he said stiffly, "but I can't bind myself by promises. Not even to you."

He pulled his arms away from her hands and turning, left the cabin. Minutes later he rode down the creek, and as he passed the open door, he saw that Rocky was sitting at the table, her head on her arms. He went on down slope, an aching emptiness in him. He had talked lightly about not needing a shotgun to marry her, too lightly. Now he knew he loved her.

His thoughts had been muddied up, living close to Peg as he had for a year and thinking he loved her. It had been cheap and he was ashamed. Peg had her way of appealing to a man; he would never forget the way she had kissed him, but that kiss had not been prompted by love. Nor could he believe she loved Dunning. It did not seem important either way.

One thought lay in his mind like a smoldering coal. Rocky did not understand why he had refused to make the promise she had asked; she would be thinking he was still in love with Peg. So he had built a wall between him and Rocky, and it might be impossible to break through to her again, to regain the intimacy that had briefly been theirs. He rode on down the twisting trail, and the night was very dark around him.

CHAPTER 14

SKY CITY

TWICE KIM lost the trail, and both times it took several minutes to find it again. Then the black mass of the timber was behind him, and he was on the flat with its sagebrush and scattered cedars. He angled southwest, leaving the trail that he and Rocky had followed the night before.

It had not rained that day at Bonham's cabin, but it had rained here, and the air was damp and tangy with sage smell. The sky was still overcast, and along the southern horizon lightning played with quick slashing thrusts that threw a weird light upon a dark earth and fled and came again.

Kim rode by instinct, for there were no stars to guide him. At times he wondered if he was going in the direction he wanted to, for in this pitch blackness a man could easily make a half circle and reverse himself. He thought with grim humor that the lights of Ganado might suddenly appear in front of him and he would discover that he was going north instead of south.

He reached the bench and let his buckskin have his head. The animal picked his way down the steep pitch, sliding a little in the mud, for apparently the rain had been heavy here. Then he was on the level grassy floor of the valley, and he came, near midnight, to a stream.

Kim reined up, listening, but there was no sound except that of some furtive night animal scurrying among the willows and the distant call of a coyote from a high point on the rim to the east. Kim had not expected to run into Dunning and the posse. Distance itself made it unlikely. They would not be in this end of the valley anyhow if they had gone to Shorty Avis' place. They would still be north of Ganado Canyon. But long experience at this game, both as the hunter and the hunted, had developed a caution in him, so he sat his saddle for several minutes, head turned to catch any sound that might drift in from the level floor of the valley.

He was certain now that he was where he wanted to be. Judging from the size of the stream, this was Pass Creek. It ran almost due south. Somewhere to the north Ganado Creek flowed into Pass Creek. There was no meandering about it here, for the tilt of the land was greater than north of town. At this place the stream moved with a steady chatter that would, a few miles to the south, become a sullen roar as it churned between the high walls of the canyon before turning west where it would eventually meet the Colorado.

Kim rode downstream, found a break in the willows, and forded the creek. Again he turned south, following the old road that now had little travel, but at one time had known a steady stream of stage-coaches moving between Sky City and Ganado.

Presently the creek dropped below the road that was now a narrow shelf carved out of the canyon wall. A solitary light showed ahead. He reined up again and listened, but he heard nothing except the steady hammering of the creek as it spewed in white-foamed fury around the huge boulders in its bed. He rode on, slowly, for he had reached Sky City.

It was a strange town, the canyon dropping away on one side, a sheer sandstone wall rising above it on the other, clinging here on a shelf that was barely wide enough for the buildings and the single street that ran in front of them. Kim had been here only once before, but he remembered it well, for Sky City was a town that, once seen, could not be easily forgotten. He pictured it now, the weathered false fronts of the deserted buildings, the long string of cabins with their windows and doors gone and their roofs falling in.

Fatty York's hotel was the only building still in use. He had a small store, a post office, and a bar along with a dining room and the few rooms on the second floor that he rented. Ed Lane made it a rule to stay out of Sky City. It was no place for a sheriff, particularly a careful one like Lane. There were still a few prospectors who haunted the high country to the south and came in twice a year to buy supplies, but the bulk of Fatty York's business was with the toughs who had beaten a posse out of New Mexico.

Kim tied in front of the hotel. There was another horse at the end of the hitch pole. Kim moved toward it, keeping off the boardwalk that was three steps above the street level. He stopped before he reached a patch of light falling into the street from the hotel windows and stood studying the horse.

It was possible that the animal belonged to a man on the dodge who had just got in, but that seemed unlikely. If that was the case, the horse would probably have been put away in York's stable down the street. It was Kim's guess that someone planned to ride out soon, possibly an HD man looking for Salty Smith.

From where Kim stood in the fringe of light he could look into the hotel lobby. Fatty York seemed to be dozing behind the desk, his bald head shiny in the lamplight. No one else was in sight. The bar and dining room were on the other side of the lobby, the interior dark.

Kim stepped up on the walk and went in. York stirred and opened his eyes. He blinked owlishly for a moment and rubbed his face, then got up and shook his head as if to clear the cobwebs from his mind. He said, "Howdy, Logan. Ain't you off your reservation?"

"Came down to look at the scenery," Kim said.

York laughed, making a show of his amusement. "Scenery, is it? Well, boy, we've got that. Maybe I should advertise."

York was a tall man, but because of his great width, he gave the impression of being shorter than he was. He wore a dark bushy mustache that made a sharp contrast with the pale skin of his face. Kim had no idea how far the man could be trusted. Bonham considered him honest, but Kim was always skeptical of those who made their living from the owl-hoot fringe of society.

"Advertising wouldn't do your business no good, would it?" Kim asked.

York laughed again, taking no offense at what Kim said. "It wouldn't for a fact. I do purty well, but a man oughtta do well, living in this hell hole." He picked up a half-chewed cigar from the desk and put it into his mouth. "Sky City, a population one human being and five thousand ghosts. Funny thing, how fellers like me and Brit Bonham up there in Ganado hang on, hoping the old camps will come back and knowing damned well they never will. Oughtta have our heads examined."

Kim made a quick study of the lobby while York talked. The store and post office were on one side, the door shut and probably locked at this time of night. On the opposite side of the lobby the door into the bar was open, a thin finger of light falling into it from the lamp on the desk. An open stairway to York's left led to the rooms upstairs. The chances were that the man who owned the other horse was not far away. He might have gone upstairs, or he might be in the bar, listening.

Casually Kim made a slow turn so that he faced the bar door, right hand at his side, left dropped casually on the desk. He asked, "How's business?"

York laughed as if everything Kim said was funny. "It ain't good, Logan. Too peaceful south of the line. What this country needs is a good bank robbery."

"I don't reckon you'd be interested in keeping a man who's wanted in Colorado?"

"Why, I might." York scratched his blob of a nose, watery eyes fixed on Kim. "I just might for a price. No price, no keep. You savvy that?"

"Sure. I've got the price all right, and I don't reckon Ed Lane's likely to be poking his nose down here. He don't want it shot off, Ed don't." Kim leaned against the desk, his mouth close to York's ear. He whispered, "I want to see Salty."

There was no change of expression on York's droopy-cheeked face. "I reckon that's right. Ed sure is a careful gent." He took the cigar out of his mouth, and said in a whisper that barely reached Kim's ears. "Pat Monroney's in the bar."

Kim nodded. He was not surprised. Monroney was one of Dunning's gun hands who had come to the valley within the last year, the kind who was fitted for this sort of job. Kim knew him slightly, but even a nodding acquaintance with the man was enough to peg him as a backshooting killer. He would murder old Salty Smith as casually as he would shoot the head off a prairie dog.

"I don't cotton much to the notion of going on across the line," Kim said. "I like it on this side, but damn it, Ganado ain't real healthy for me."

York's big laugh boomed out again, "I heard about that. Well, you'll be as safe here as if you was in church. Good grub three times a day, plenty of whiskey, and a damned fine bed. Fifty dollars a day."

"Fair enough," Kim said. "Let's have a drink on it. Then

I'll see how good that bed of yours is. Been riding so long I wore calluses on my saddle."

"Now that's a hell of a place to get calluses." This time York didn't laugh. He put the cigar back into his mouth and chewed on it. Then he said, "Maybe you'd better go on up and start trying the bed. We'll have the drink in the morning."

Monroney appeared in the doorway. "I'll drink with Logan, Fatty. We'll drink to Salty Smith."

York picked up the lamp and waddled into the bar. "All right, if that's what you want, only it's a hell of a thing to drink at this time of night."

Monroney stepped back into the bar. As Kim followed York through the door, Monroney gave him a wink. "Fatty figgers we ain't good pay. Stingy, that's what he is. Fifty dollars a day is standard rate in this boar's nest. I've had some friends who holed up here. It ain't right. They knock a bank over, take all the risks, and then they have to give what they've made to this keg of lard who don't do nothing but rustle grub and hand out a bottle of Valley Tan now and then."

"Don't be so damned smart, friend," York growled sullenly. "Ain't no law making you stay here."

"I ain't staying long." Monroney picked up the bottle and glasses that York had set on the bar and moved to the table. "Sit down, Logan."

Kim followed, wondering about this. Monroney was a knot-headed man with a scarred face and a pair of beady eyes set too close together astride a beaky nose. He was the one man in Dunning's outfit that Kim regarded with high contempt. If it had been Tonto Miles or Phil Martin, he would have come out of the bar with his gun smoking, but that would have entailed some danger, and Monroney was the sort who avoided danger if he could. It was Kim's guess that he had some kind of a trick up his sleeve that he considered foolproof, or he would have remained under cover.

Monroney poured the drinks and shoved one glass across the table. Kim sat down across the table from him, watching Monroney's hands. He said, "So we're drinking to Salty Smith."

"That's right." Monroney's thin lips held what was meant to be a genial smile. "You know, Logan, you fooled us, which same includes Dunning. We figgered you was just bluff, making all that big talk about Clawhammer hanging onto every foot of range that old Sam had claimed. Well, we know different. Tonto found out how good you are with a six."

Monroney had his drink and put the empty glass down.

"I kind o' liked Tonto, but the way I hear it, he had his chance. Well, you see how it is. Talk don't really hurt nothing, but it's different now. If you was smart, you'd get across the line."

Kim waited, saying nothing, waiting for the move that he knew Monroney planned to make. This was like the man, talking with cool confidence, very casually, all the time hoping that Kim's nerves were knotting. There was a moment of silence, broken only by York's heavy breathing from where he stood behind the bar.

Then Monroney, still casual, poured another drink and lifted the glass to his mouth, right hand dropping below the table top. Kim came up out of his chair like a thin spring uncoiling. He heaved the table over on Monroney, his glass and bottle spilling to the floor, and backed away, drawing his .44.

The HD man, not expecting this, fell sideways and rolled and came up with his gun. Kim fired, getting Monroney in the chest. Monroney's shot was a split second slow and went wide. Kim let go with another shot, smashing Monroney's gun arm.

That was all. Monroney lay flat on his back, staring up at Kim and cursing him in a low, wicked tone, the knowledge of death haunting his beady eyes. York came across the room, still breathing hard. He said, "You ain't smart, Monroney. Not half as smart as you allowed."

"A man's smart if he makes it." Monroney's left hand gripped his shirt front. His fingers straightened and he raised his hand and looked at the blood. "He ain't smart if he don't make it. So I ain't smart."

Then, with the last strength that was in him, he grabbed the gun that lay beside him and lifted it. Kim took one quick step and kicked the gun out of Monroney's hand, sending it clattering across the floor. Monroney fell back, eyes glazed, blood showing on his lips. He took one hard, sawing breath, then he was still.

"First time I was ever glad to see a man die," York said. "He was fixing to drill you under the table when he took that drink."

"I know," Kim said.

"He got the drop on me," York said bitterly. "I ain't much good with a gun. Don't have to be. The boys all figger they'll need me some day. If Monroney had drilled me, one of 'em would have got him. He should have known that."

Kim moved toward the lobby, saying, "Come on. I want to see Salty."

York picked up the lamp and tromped through the door. He set the lamp on the desk and faced Kim, chewing fiercely on a cigar. He asked, "What do you want with him?"

100

"He's gonna answer a question."

"Look, Logan. Salty's a friend of mine." York motioned with a wide inclusive gesture. "I've always been too fat to be good for anything. I mean, like punching cows or working in a mine. Well, I didn't have much money when I came here. Salty took a liking to me and staked me to this. Now I'm returning the favor. I'm protecting him. Savvy?"

"I didn't come here to hurt him," Kim said quietly. "It's the other way around. As long as Dunning's riding high around here, Salty's in a tight. If I can keep my neck out of a rope long enough, I'll get Dunning. Then Salty can go back home."

Still York hesitated. He said finally, "It ain't that simple. Not to me. I dunno what's going on up the valley, but I do know you're with Clawhammer. Why don't you go back and do your fighting where you oughtta?"

"They want me for murder," Kim answered. "I can't do no fighting till I clean that up. Salty can do it for me."

"How do you figger Salty knows anything?"

"He wouldn't be here if he didn't know who killed Yuma Bill."

Sweat broke out across the fat man's face. He kept chewing on his cigar, and time ran on until the seconds piled up into a minute. Kim, sensing the agony of uncertainty that was in the man, said patiently, "I told you I wasn't here to hurt the old man, York. I aim to do him a favor as well as myself."

"All right," York said. "I'll go get him, but if you lay a hand on him, I'll black your name from here to hell."

York took the lamp and started up the stairs, the steps creaking under his great weight. Kim followed. York called back over his shoulder, "Stay there. I told you I'd get him."

"I'll tag along."

York turned, holding the lamp high, its light falling across Kim's dark, stubble-covered face. "My word goes around here. Savvy?"

"You could get him out while I waited."

"Damn it, I . . ."

"Ever feel a rope on your neck?" Kim asked.

"No."

"I've got one waiting for me in Ganado if I let Salty get away from me. Now go on."

York turned and went on. Reaching the hall, he moved along it in his lumbering walk to the back room. He tapped on the door, calling, "Salty."

"What's wrong?" the old man quavered.

York pushed the door open and went in. "Nothing now, Salty. Everything's all right." He set the lamp on the bureau and turned to face Smith. "There was plenty wrong while

101

ago. Monroney was here. He was aiming to make me tell him where you was, but Logan came in and drilled him."

Kim stood in the doorway, looking at Smith who was eyeing him in abject fear. He cried out, "Go away, Logan. I don't know nothing."

"Logan ain't here to hurt you, Salty," York said, "but Monroney would have if Logan hadn't got him. You owe him something, so you'd best tell him what he wants to know."

Smith looked down at the floor. "I don't know nothing."

"You know who killed Yuma Bill," Kim said. "Dunning wants to hang me for it."

Smith's gnarled hands fisted. He sat on the edge of the bed, a dirty bearded old man smelling of stale sweat and cheap whiskey. Kim, seeing him this way, found it hard to believe that he had once been a wealthy man and one of the town fathers of Ganado.

"I don't know nothing," Smith said, still staring at the floor.

"You want to go back home," York urged. "Only way to fix it so you can is to tell Logan."

"He won't fix nothing," Smith shrilled. "Logan's a Clawhammer man. He'll kill me. Monroney didn't have nothing against me."

"You're wrong, Salty," York said patiently. "I'm your friend. You've got to believe me when I tell you that Monroney would have killed me and you both. He's the one who wanted to shut your mouth."

Kim crossed the room and sat down beside Smith. "Phil Martin claims I did it. You and me know different. I'm not working for Clawhammer any more. That makes a hell of a lot of difference, Salty."

"You're lying."

"No, Peg fired me. Sometimes a man don't know who his friends are. Bonham helped bust me out of jail. Bonham's your friend, too."

"A good friend," Smith whispered. "It's you I don't know about. I figgered you'd kill me if I talked."

"No," Kim said with the patience he would have used with a child, "it's Dunning's bunch that want to kill you. I've got to clear myself. Then I can help you."

Smith turned bloodshot eyes to York. "I'd like to go home, Fatty. I'd like to go home."

"Tell him," York urged. "It ain't like we figgered, or Monroney wouldn't have come here tonight."

"All right, I'll tell him." Smith's hands gripped his knees. He leaned forward, shoulders sagging. "I was fishing. See? I wasn't paying no attention to anything. I was just above my

102

cabin a piece. I had a bite and I was trying to get that trout out from under a willow when I heard a shot. I looked up. One feller was on the ground. This other feller had a smoking gun in his hand. He stooped down and yanked off the dead man's money belt."

"Who was it?" Kim asked.

Smith drew back, suspicion clouding his mind again. "You're Clawhammer. I don't trust you."

"I'm not working for Clawhammer," Kim told him again, "but it wouldn't make any difference if I was. You see, Monroney wouldn't have been here to shut your mouth if it had been a Clawhammer man who killed Yuma Bill."

"But I saw what I saw," Smith shouted. "It was Clawhammer, I tell you. It was . . . it was . . ." He turned his eyes to York. "Get me a drink, Fatty. Seems like I can't remember nothing."

"No drink," Kim said, impatience crowding him. "Not till he answers my question."

"It . . ." Smith got up. "It was . . ." He backed across the room, watching Kim with worried uncertainty. Then he blurted, "It was Dutch Heinz."

Kim forgot to breathe. He had the same feeling that he'd had when Rocky had told him Peg was in love with Dunning. It didn't seem possible that Dutch Heinz had killed Yuma Bill, not with Dunning and Martin trying to protect the killer. Then he remembered other things: Heinz wanting to rob Yuma Bill that night in Peg's kitchen, of Peg's pressing need for money, Yuma Bill's saying he had heard someone ride out of the yard that night. Kim still didn't have all the threads, but he had enough to form the pattern. Dunning and Heinz and Peg were together.

"Surprised?" York asked.

"Plenty."

Kim got up from the bed, watching Salty Smith who had backed against the wall and was staring at him with the soul-deep fear of a man who thinks he may still be murdered.

"What are you gonna do?" York asked.

"Can't let Smith go back," Kim said thoughtfully. "Too dangerous. You'll have to keep him for a while. Till you get word that Dunning's finished. Then he can go home. You fetch that bottle and bring up a pen and paper. Salty's gonna write out a statement of what he saw, and I'll shove it down Ed Lane's throat."

"The way I heard it, Martin claimed you . . ."

"You heard right," Kim said, "but now that I know who did beef Yuma Bill, Martin's gonna change his story." Kim jerked his head at the door. "Go get that bottle. Salty deserves it."

CHAPTER 15

THE TORCH

It was mid-morning when Kim reached Ganado. He was sleepy and hungry and more tired than he had ever been before in his life. Still, food and sleep must wait. He had no way of knowing where the posse was, but by this time every member would be worn to a frazzle if it had kept on the move.

The question in Kim's mind was whether the posse had returned to town. Ed Lane had probably caught up with Dunning and the others. The trick would be to get him and Phil Martin together. If Kim could do that, he was reasonably sure he could clear himself.

Avoiding the business block, Kim rode into town on a side street that, like most of Ganado's streets, was flanked by deserted houses. If he was seen, there was no indication of it. The entire town seemed as empty of life as the empty buildings facing the street.

Ed Lane lived in a white house one block east of the courthouse. Kim turned into an alley and came to the rear of the sheriff's place. The only sign of life was the column of smoke rising from the chimney. Dismounting, Kim led his buckskin into Lane's barn and left him in the second stall so he would not be seen by anyone casually passing the sheriff's house. Lane's horse was in the first stall, and judging from his appearance, he had been ridden long and hard.

Kim walked up the path to the back door, hoping that Lane would be inside. He knocked, and Lane's housekeeper opened the door. Without waiting for an invitation, Kim shoved past her into the house.

"I want to see Lane," Kim said.

The woman began to swell up. She said in a strident voice, "You can't force your way into a house like this. Ed will arrest you for breaking and entering. Now get out before I call him."

"I've already entered, and I'll sure break something if I don't see Ed. Where is he?"

The woman backed away toward the stove, apparently recognizing him, for she was afraid. "You're . . . you're Kim Logan, ain't you?"

"That's right. Where's Lane?"

"You're wanted for murder. Now you've come here to kill . . ."

"Shut up. I'm not going to hurt you. Or Ed if he behaves, but I don't figure on standing here all morning asking you where he is."

"He's asleep. He just got in a little while ago."

"Looks like he'll be waking up pronto. Which room?"

She kept back away from Kim until she stood with her back pressed against the sink. Now she put her hands behind her and gripped it. "Don't you come no closer. Don't you lay a hand on me."

The woman was a middle-aged blonde, as dumpy as a filled wool sack. Kim said mildly, "You're exaggerating your talents, ma'am. Ed's the one I want. Now unless you want him hurt, you stay right there, peaceful like."

He stepped into the living room. One door opened into the parlor; the door on the other side of the room was closed. Kim opened it and looked in. He had guessed right. It was Lane's bedroom. He lay crosswise on the bed in the manner of a man who had fallen there and gone to sleep at once, too tired to move. He had not even bothered to undress. Only his coat, Stetson, and gun belt were on the chair beside the bed.

Kim pulled the chair back so Lane could not reach his gun. Then he put up the blind and the morning sunshine cut squarely across the sheriff's face.

"Time to get up and start the day, Ed," Kim said, shaking Lane.

The sheriff turned over, gave a great gurgling snore, the corners of his mouth working, and kept on sleeping. Kim shook him again, this time with considerable violence, and Lane reared up, eyes blinking in the sunlight.

"No sense sleeping all day, Ed," Kim said. "Time to get up."

Recognition struck Lane then, and his eyes became bright with fear. His face and the front of his shiny bald head turned white; he gave out a hoarse yelp and rolled to the side of his bed, both hands reaching out in a wild grab for his gun. The chair wasn't where he had left it, and because there was nothing to sustain him, he fell out of bed, hitting the floor with a great clatter and shaking a picture on the wall above him.

"Now what do you know about that?" Kim stood with one foot on a chair rung, a hand dropped on the gun belt dangling over the back. "Somebody moved that chair. Ain't that a hell of a note?"

Lane sat up, rubbed his eyes and shook his head. He blurted, "What do you want?"

"Heard you was looking for me, so I came in. Funny thing, Ed. You don't seem real pleased about it."

"Sure, sure. You're showing sense now. Too bad Bonham didn't show as much when he helped bust you out. I'll have him and that Della Naylor keeping you company behind bars afore the day's over."

Lane got to his feet and started toward the chair. He stopped abruptly when Kim held up a hand. "You don't need your cutter. I've got a surprise for you. I didn't plug Yuma Bill."

"You've said that before, but a jury . . ."

"We don't even need a jury." Kim pulled a folded piece of paper from his coat pocket and held it up for Lane to see, then replaced it. "I've got a statement signed by an eyewitness. You know, Ed, it's gonna be real dangerous, bringing in that hombre that beefed Yuma Bill."

"I won't have to go very far," Lane flung at him. "Not with you standing right here, and I'll have Bonham . . ."

"Did you see Bonham help me out of jail?"

"Hell, somebody slugged me when Della . . ."

Lane stopped, red-faced. Kim laughed. "You sure made a fool out of yourself. What do you think Johnny's gonna do when you tell folks you got slugged when you was kissing his wife?" Kim shook his head. "You'd better keep mum. Ed, you do what I want you to and I'll keep still about you and Del. I'll be saving your life, you know. Johnny sure is a jealous hombre."

"All right. What do you want?"

"We'll take a walk to Doc's place and see Phil Martin. I've got a notion he'll change his yarn."

For a moment Lane stood there, blinking idiotically, wanting no part of this, but unable to find a way out. He said sourly, "Gimme my coat. I need a chaw of tobacco."

Kim tossed the coat to Lane who slipped into it, took a plug of tobacco out of his pocket, and gnawed off a mouthful. He said thickly, "Gimme my gun belt. I'd look naked without it."

Kim lifted the gun from holster and removed the shells, then handed the belt and gun to Lane. "You had your fun pushing me down the street the other day. Now I'll have some. Don't load that iron. Walk out ahead of me and keep going till we get to Doc's drugstore."

Lane swore bitterly, but he obeyed. As he crossed the living room, his housekeeper called, "What's he doing to you, Ed?"

"Nothing. We've got some business to attend to."

When they were outside, Kim said, "I thought the posse rode off and left you."

"I caught up with 'em at Clawhammer. I figgered you'd go there."

"Where's Dunning and his outfit?"

"They stopped at Clawhammer. Sleeping, I reckon. We couldn't find you, so Dunning stayed there and the rest of us came back to town. Johnny had to go out on the stage and Luke Haines allowed he'd better get back to see how his wife was."

"Ain't it funny Dunning would stop at Clawhammer?"

"Looked funny to me," Lane admitted, "but they was all in. Needed sleep, Dunning said."

They walked in silence then, Kim thinking that this was further proof of what Rocky had said about Peg and Dunning. They turned into the drugstore. Doc Frazee stood behind the counter, looking tired and sleepy, and even surprise at seeing Kim did not change the expression on his bony face.

"Well, Ed, I see you caught your man," Frazee said. "Shall we hang him this morning, or wait till Dunning gets back to town?"

Lane glowered, saying nothing. Kim said, "Got anything for a sour disposition, Doc?"

"Sure, but you can get it cheaper in the Belle Union."

"Come on," Lane said irritably. "Get on with the business."

"How's Martin?" Kim asked.

"Purty sick. I've been up and down all night with him. The damned fool should have stayed in bed, but no, he figured he was so tough he didn't need to do what he was told."

"I want to see him," Kim said. "He's gonna tell who beefed Yuma Bill. I've got a statement from Salty Smith, so I figured if Martin's story jibes with Smith's, even Lane will get it through his noggin that I ain't the man he wants."

Frazee stood motionless for a moment, stroking his goatee. He said finally, "Let me handle this, Kim. I've got a scheme I've been waiting to use till Ed was here to listen."

The medico led the way to his office in the back of the store building. He went into a side room, motioning for Kim and Lane to wait.

"How do you feel, Phil?" Frazee asked.

"You know damned well," Martin groaned. "I'm burning up."

"They tell me hell's hot, too. I reckon you'll be finding out before long, but it might ease your conscience if you'd tell me who drilled Yuma Bill."

"I'm sick," Martin grunted, "but I ain't sick enough to admit I'm a liar."

Frazee put a hand on Martin's forehead and jerked it

107

away "I could fry an egg right there, Phil. I'll stir up something to take your fever down."

Frazee poured water into a glass, dropped a spoonful of white powder into it, and stirred lustily. He stepped back to the cot. "Here, Phil. Drink this."

Frazee got a hand behind Martin's head and tilted it up so the man could drink. Martin emptied the glass and Frazee stepped back, grinning. He said, "Phil, there's times when a sawbones has to stick his nose into business that ain't rightfully his. That's just what I done. Logan didn't beef that hombre. You know who did. Now the way I see it, that makes you guilty of murder if Logan hangs, but there ain't no court hereabouts that'll see justice done. So I took care of it myself."

"What're you driving at?"

"I executed you. That was poison you just drank. Tasted awful, didn't it? In about a minute you'll feel a tingling in your fingers and toes. Then it'll be in your hands and feet. Pretty soon it'll go up into your arms and legs. When it hits your heart, wham, you're dead."

"You're lying."

"Think so? Well, all I've got to say is that I wish I had Hank Dunning here so I could lie to him the same way."

Martin must have believed him then, for he cried out, "Do something, damn it. You just can't stand there and let me die."

"Getting into your legs, ain't it? It'll be up in your arms. First they tingle, then they'll get stiff. Pretty soon . . ."

Martin lifted himself on his one good arm, yelling, "Shut up, damn you, and do something."

"You'll make your fever worse, carrying on thataway," Frazee said reprovingly. He took a bottle down from a shelf and filled a small glass with amber liquid. "This is the antidote, Phil. I aim to get the truth out of you or kill you. Tell me who drilled Yuma Bill and you get the antidote."

"Go to hell," Martin breathed, and fell back on the cot.

"Well sir, I didn't think you were that big a fool," Frazee said contemptuously. "You're lying to get rid of Logan, and you're doing it because Dunning told you to. Now ain't that a fine thing to die for?"

"Go to hell," Martin said again.

"You're the one going to hell. My conscience won't hurt me for sending you there. I'm trying to save an innocent man's life. Do you think that what Dunning told you to do is enough to kill yourself for? Getting it in your legs and arms now, ain't you? When it hits your heart . . ."

"All right," Martin screamed. "It was Heinz."

"Now that's better. Here's your . . ."

108

"Wait a minute," Kim called from the door. "Did Dutch get the money?"

"Sure, sure. Hank and that Cody woman rigged it. She said he'd have all the dinero in a shoe box. Forty thousand. Said the old gent was gonna keep the dinero while you rode into town, but you crossed 'em up when you took the box. Dutch couldn't find it, so he figured the old man had the dinero on him. That's how he found the money belt. Now gimme that stuff, Doc."

"Here you are," Frazee said.

Martin hoisted himself up on his good arm and drained the glass. "Whiskey," he yelled. "Nothing but your damned cheap whiskey." He threw the glass against the wall. "You lying son! When I get out of here, I'll . . ."

"Cool down, boy," Frazee said. "That's no way to act after my saving your life. Whiskey is a good antidote for a lot of things. Look at all the fellers who use it."

Frazee walked out, leaving Martin staring after him, uncertain whether he had been tricked or not. The medico shut the door, winking at Kim. "If properly used, bicarbonate of soda and imagination can do more to change men's lives than all the pills a doctor can roll."

Kim handed Smith's statement to Frazee. "You know Salty Smith's handwriting, Doc?"

"Sure. Nobody could forge that old fool's scrawling. Not even a barnyard hen." He glanced at the paper and nodding, handed it to Lane. "It tallies, Ed."

Lane studied the paper a moment and then glanced up at Kim. "Where is Smith?"

"He's safe. You go get Dutch. Salty'll be here to testify at his trial."

"Where is he?" Lane asked again.

"I wouldn't trust you as far as I could throw you by the hair on your head," Kim said bluntly. "If Smith was dead, Martin could go back on his story, so I'll do all I can to keep Smith alive."

Lane wheeled toward the door. Frazee called, "Ed." Lane made a slow turn to face the medico and stood glowering at him. Frazee said, "Ed, you're a tinhorn politician. We all know that, but if you haven't got the guts it takes to go after Dutch Heinz, you'd better turn your star in."

"I don't get it," Lane shouted. "I tell you I don't get it. Heinz has been with Clawhammer ever since Sam Cody drove into the valley. It don't make sense that Dunning would protect him and try to hang Logan."

"I'm not working for Clawhammer," Kim said in a low tone. "That's the difference."

"I still don't savvy."

"You don't need to savvy. Are you going after Heinz?"

Lane stood in the doorway, trembling, sweat breaking through the pores of his skin. "I'll go look for him," he muttered.

"You'd better find him," Frazee said. "Things are changing around here. For the better, too. A few more funerals will just about clean things up."

Again Lane turned and this time Frazee let him go. When he had left the drugstore, Kim said, "He's a dead man if he goes after Heinz."

"Or a man without a job if he don't," Frazee said. "He can't make up his mind which way to jump."

Kim walked to the door and leaned against the jamb, shoulders slack. He yawned and rubbed his face. "Guess I'll get some breakfast and sleep till Christmas." He yawned again. "Thanks, Doc. I'm so damned near all in I ain't got it through my noggin that I don't have to keep ducking the law."

"No need to thank me, Kim." Frazee's bony face was very grave. "You know, the other morning when I was standing in front of the bank, I wasn't much different from Fred Galt and Luke Haines. Kind o' felt that the country had gone to the dogs and I didn't give a damn. Then you fetched in that dinero and well, things began looking different."

"Yuma Bill was the one who made things look different," Kim said.

"To you," Frazee agreed. "It's like a chain. But it was some different with me. I'd been rotting inside for years. I'd seen this country boom and I'd seen it die. I've seen a few honest folks and a lot of crooked ones. Why, if I could collect all the money I've got coming, I'd be a rich man. I've got enough, though. The thing was I got to talking to Brit, about what the country used to be like. We want to see it come back and I think it will. Trouble is, it ain't good for folks to live with ghosts. A lot of us have been gripped by the dead hand of the past till we've been paralyzed."

"It ain't the dead hand of the past that's been bothering me," Kim said, and left the medico's office.

He had flapjacks at the Chinaman's, and taking his horse out of Lane's barn, rode to the livery stable. It was a grim sort of joke, he thought, that he had cheated the lynch mob by riding out of town on Shorty Avis's black, for Shorty hated him with only a little less bitterness than Hank Dunning did. He told the stableman to keep the gelding until Shorty or Rocky came for him, stopped to talk to his buckskin, and left the stable.

Kim went to the bank. What Doc Frazee had said about being gripped by the dead hand of the past had given him an

110

idea. Charlie Bemis froze behind the teller's wicket when he saw Kim. He blurted, "You loco, Kim? The posse just got back this morning. They'll . . ."

"No they won't. I'm gonna laugh in Fred Galt's face soon as I get some sleep. Brit back yet?"

Bemis nodded. "He's in his office. Lane . . ."

"He don't want me." Kim said, and stepping through the gate at the end of the counter, walked on back to Bonham's office.

Kim knocked, and opened the door at the banker's. "Come in." He said, "Don't get excited, Brit. The law don't want me. Charlie had himself a conniption when I came in."

Bonham had started to get up, his face paling when he saw who it was. Then he dropped back into his chair, his body going slack, and it seemed to Kim that his shoulders were more stooped than ever.

"Let's hear the yarn afore I die of heart failure," Bonham said, filling his pipe, eyes dropping to his tobacco pouch.

Kim told him what had happened, then asked, "What about Rocky?"

"She lit out for home. Mighty worried about you, too. You'd best ride out there as soon as you get some sleep."

"I aim to." Kim canted his chair back against the wall and rolled a smoke. "What do you want most, Brit?"

Bonham lit his pipe, blinking as the smoke rolled up around his face. He took the pipestem out of his mouth. "Now that's a hell of a question."

"Sure is," Kim agreed. "Maybe it's because I'm so sleepy that my head's spinning, but I think I've got an idea. Strikes me that some of you old timers, you and Doc for instance, want to see this country come back before you go over the range."

Bonham pulled on his pipe a moment. He said, "That's right, but who's gonna bring it back? I've got a little claim up there back of my cabin, but it ain't gonna be no bonanza. Same with Doc."

"Mines come and go, Brit. Trouble with you and Doc is that you saw this country when it had its boom, so you figure that another strike is the only way to bring it back. You're wrong, Brit. The grass will always be here."

Bonham gestured impatiently. "We've had cows in this valley ever since Sam Cody brought his herd in. Before that even, but it didn't bring no big prosperity."

"And I'll tell you why. Clawhammer and HD are both big outfits. It's the little fry who'll bring the country back, fellows like Shorty Avis that Sam Cody ran off the creek. If this range was handled right, there'd be enough grass for fifty outfits. Think about that, Brit. It means business for every-

111

body, more'n you'd ever have with two big spreads and a few dinky ones on the mesa."

Bonham shook his head. "There's a gent named Hank Dunning . . ."

"Won't be long." Kim's face was bone-hard. "I'll attend to Dunning, and I'll attend to Heinz if Lane don't."

Bonham puffed for a moment in silence. Then he said, "You've been a fool for luck, although I've always claimed that it takes a real good man to have good luck. Anyhow, you might pull it off, but no matter what happens to Dunning, there's still Peg."

"You've got her notes."

"Yeah, and it won't hurt my conscience to close her out after what's happened." Bonham studied his pipe, eyes almost lidded shut. "But I had the notion you were in love with Peg."

Kim's face reddened. "Rub it in. I guess Rocky called it right. I was in love with Clawhammer, not Peg. Anyhow, I'm seeing it straight now. It's Rocky I'm in love with, and I'll prove it to her if I stay here a million years."

"Might take that long. It's my guess that Rocky's gonna be hard to convince."

"I'll do it if it takes that million years. Now you've got forty thousand dollars you don't know what to do with. My idea is for you to loan it out to the little fry. Let 'em start in the valley again. If we don't have talk of a range war, there'll be others who'll move in."

Bonham leaned back, puffing steadily on his pipe, eyes on the ceiling. "You're dreaming, boy, just dreaming, and there's a lot to be done before what you're talking about can be anything but dreams."

"We'll do 'em."

"Kim," Bonham said slowly, "there's one thing I can't get out of my mind. You've been a fiddle-footed drifter. How do I know you've changed?"

Kim got up. "You don't. Go ahead and keep Yuma's money in your safe till it rots, but I'm betting on one thing. When you go over the range, Yuma will be standing beside St. Peter and he'll blackball you before you get through the pearly gates."

Kim swung around and would have stalked out if Bonham hadn't said, "That might happen. I'll make you a deal. Interested?"

"Maybe," Kim answered, turning back.

"A lot of things can change a man," Bonham said, "but a woman's one of the best. That's how it was with Yuma. Like I told you, he was mighty damned ornery once. Bought a big grant in New Mexico and sold land to settlers that

112

wasn't no good for farming. They failed and moved on and the land went back to him. Then he sold it over again. He piled up a lot of money, then he fell in love with one of them farmer's girls, and she made him into the Yuma Bill you knew. By that time he couldn't give the money back to the fellers he'd taken it from, so he came up to the Arkansas Valley and since then he's done his damnedest to help other people with that money."

Bonham rose and kicked back his chair. "Kim, what you've said is right in line with what Yuma Bill would want done with his money. You see, even after his wife died, he went right on like he had been. If you'd marry Peg, you wouldn't be no different than when you rode into the valley, but if it's Rocky you marry, you'll be different. I'll gamble on that."

"What's your deal?" Kim asked in a dry brittle tone.

"The day you marry Rocky, I'll loan that forty thousand dollars."

"You've made a deal," Kim said, and left the bank.

He was angry, as angry as he could be at a man who had helped save his life, but as he crossed the street to the hotel, he found that he could not remain angry at Brit Bonham. The banker had always been the little rancher's friend; he was Rocky's friend. If his and Bonham's positions had been reversed and he was looking at Kim Logan's record, he would have figured on the future exactly as the banker had.

Kim took a room and climbed the stairs, thinking of Rocky. Without her, his future would be little different from his past. It was, he knew now, not the kind of future he wanted. He pulled off his coat and gun belt, tossed his Stetson on the bureau, and fell across the bed. His last thought was of Rocky and how she had changed so many things in the last few days.

It was dark when Kim woke. His door was open and a thin pencil of light from the bracket lamp in the hall fell half across his room. He wasn't sure, in that first moment of sleep-fogged consciousness, what had wakened him, but he thought someone was shaking him and talking to him. He turned toward the wall, hoping he was dreaming.

No dream. It came again, a slender hand on his shoulder shaking him with nagging insistence. A woman's voice beat against his sleep-numbed brain, "Wake up, Kim. Wake up."

He sat up, knuckling his eyes and shaking his head. Then he saw it was Della Naylor. He yawned and mumbled, "Howdy, Del. Thought you was a dream."

"And I thought you were dead. Are you awake enough to listen?"

"Sure," Kim said, suddenly conscious of the urgency that was in her voice. "What's wrong?"

"Everything, Kim. The Avis place was burned last night and Shorty Avis was beaten up. Doc's on his way out there now, but I'm afraid he's too late."

CHAPTER 16

~~~~~~

FAITH AND DOUBT

KIM swung his feet to the floor, his brain as numb as if he had been struck on the head. This was a nightmare. It had to be. When he had cleared himself of Yuma Bill's murder, he had thought that the immediate problem had been taken care of He had never been a man to do a job that belonged to the law. Arresting Dutch Heinz was the sheriff's responsibility, and that, Kim had supposed, was the only other chore which needed to be done at once.

Now, staring at Della's face, pinched with worry, he knew that the worst fears of the mesa ranchers would soon be realized, that this blow at Shorty Avis was meant as an example of what would happen to the rest if they didn't get out of the country.

Kim rose and buckled on his gun belt. He asked, "Who did it?"

"We don't know. Shorty's been unconscious. Rocky stopped at our place after she left Bonham's cabin. Then she went home and found her dad. Everything they own is gone except their cattle."

"They'll lose their beef, too," Kim said somberly, "unless something happens to change Dunning's mind."

Kim put on his hat and coat and turned to the door. Della cried out, "Kim."

He swung back to face her. "What?"

"Rocky doesn't know I'm here. I mean, well, it was my idea. I came to get Doc and he told me you'd found out about Heinz. I got to wondering what you'd do. There's nothing to hold you in the valley now that you've lost your job with Clawhammer."

It was natural enough for her to think that. Probably her father, Abe Fawcett, and the rest of the mesa ranchers would think the same thing. He was a gunslinger, they'd say, and when he lost his job, he'd ride on. A year ago he would have done exactly that. He might have a week ago. But as Doc Frazee said, the events of the last few days formed a chain going back to Yuma Bill who had owed a debt to Brit Bonham. When Kim had delivered the money, Bonham had owed him. Now it was Kim who owed a debt to Della Naylor and Rocky Avis. That would have been enough to make him stay even if he had not loved Rocky.

"I've got another job to do," Kim said. "I aim to hang around awhile."

She came toward him, the faint light from the hall touching her troubled face. He had never supposed she had a serious thought in her rattle-brained head. When she had married Johnny Naylor, folks said they were two of a kind, reckless and wild, and they belonged together.

But Della had changed just as everything on this range was changing, for people and their relationships were distorted by the gods of evil that had been loosed upon the valley when Hank Dunning and Peg Cody had opened Pandora's box. Now Kim wondered whether Della and Johnny did belong together. She had grown up and Johnny had lagged behind.

"There's another thing, Kim," Della said. "Yesterday Heinz saw every rancher on the east mesa. He's giving us till sunset tomorrow to get out."

"He gave Shorty a warning like that the other day."

She nodded. "Sam Cody drove us out of the valley, and Heinz thinks he can drive us off the mesa just as easy. He said that if we wanted to sell, to be in town tomorrow afternoon and Peg would buy our land and cattle. If we didn't, we wouldn't get anything."

Kim turned toward the door again, saying, "Come on."

She followed him along the hall and down the stairs, and as they crossed the lobby, he asked, "Where's your horse?"

"In front of the drugstore."

"Ride over to the stable."

"Where are we going?"

He was on the boardwalk in front of the hotel when she asked that. He wheeled to face her. "That's the craziest question I ever heard. We're going up on the mesa and we'll get your neighbors together. If they want to run, there's nothing on God's earth anybody can do for 'em, but if they want to fight, we'll show Dutch Heinz a thing or two."

"They won't run, Kim," she said with grim certainty. "They've had one meeting. That was the night after Shorty had his warning. They saw that this was coming."

"Then we'll fight."

"It's not as simple as that, Kim. Try to understand. Rocky and I believe in you. So does Frazee and Brit Bonham. But Dad and the rest don't know all that's happened. To them you're still Peg Cody's snake stomper."

"Then we'll have to do some arguing," he said, and went on to the stable.

They took the stage road out of town, keeping a steady, ground-eating pace, and saying nothing. They passed the Clawhammer road and within the hour reached the road that led to Indian Springs. It was little more than a trail and was seldom used except by Shorty Avis and Abe Fawcett who followed it when they came to town. Beyond their places it climbed to the top of the slick-rock rim through a narrow break and ran on through the aspens and spruce to where it joined the stage road just west of the pass. Kim had followed the upper end of this road when he had brought Yuma Bill to the Avis place.

The bulk of the mesa ranchers lived north of the stage road, for that part of the mesa had the best grass, and it was natural that they would go there when Sam Cody had driven them out of the valley. This sudden and violent move on Heinz's part must have been supported by Dunning.

It was Kim's guess that Dunning and his tough crew had been with Heinz when Shorty Avis was beaten and his buildings burned. There could be but one answer. Kim's thoughts came back to the same place they had been many times since Rocky had told him that Peg and Dunning were in love. At least they had thrown in together and were planning a big expansion of their herds. Only a frantic need for more summer range would explain a raid like this.

The country south of Ganado Canyon was not used by any of the ranchers, for it was poor graze all the way to the New Mexico line where it became a maze of impenetrable gorges. As it stood now, Clawhammer was obliged to seek summer range in the high country between the mesa and the divide where the season was comparatively short. In the past it had been sufficient because Clawhammer beef had been held in the valley most of the year, but the valley grass would not be enough if the Clawhammer herd was doubled.

It seemed incredible, but it must be this way. The much talked about fight between Clawhammer and HD had been faked, a smoke screen to hide Peg's and Dunning's real intent. A few shots had been fired across the creek; there had been a good deal of maneuvering when the two outfits had hit Ganado the same day. Supposedly Kim's reputation had held Dunning back, but all the time Peg had known Dunning would not make a serious attack. That was why she had been so sure she would be safe when she stayed at home with no one to protect her but old Limpy.

At last logic forced Kim to the conclusion that his pride had kept him from reaching before. He had been a tool, a small but essential cog in Peg's scheming. It was the reason she had hired him; it was the reason she had paid him the high wages she had.

There were still some facts that Kim did not have and he needed them to bring the muddled pattern out clearly, but this much he could no longer doubt. She had told him she was ambitious; she aimed to be big, so big that the valley would be hers. She had said that when she needed the mesa, the little ranchers would go. Her time of need, he thought, grimly, must have come very quickly after his talk with her the night he had brought Yuma Bill to Clawhammer.

Apparently Yuma's coming had forced Peg and Dunning into the open. They had planned to steal his money. That was why Phil Martin and his men had crossed the creek. It was why Peg told Heinz that Yuma Bill would be at Smith's cabin with the money. There it was, as plain and brutal a pattern of robbery and murder as Kim had ever seen. A man could not have fooled him, but Peg had for the simple reason that he had wanted to believe in her.

One thing still bothered Kim. Doubling the Clawhammer and HD herds would take money. The ten thousand Dutch Heinz had stolen from Yuma Bill would not be enough. They must hold another trump card they had not played, or they wouldn't have started pushing the mesa ranchers so soon as they had.

It was after midnight when Kim and Della reached the bench. They climbed the steep pitch to the mesa and pulled up to blow their horses. Kim asked, "If you knew the law didn't want me and you thought there was nothing here to hold me, how come you bothered to wake me up?"

"I had to be sure," she answered. "Rocky and me invested quite a bit in you. I guess Rocky had her own reasons, but mine were pretty simple. I just figured that when the chips were down, you'd have to be on our side."

"I won't be much help if your bunch won't trust me."

"That worried me more than anything else." Leather squeaked as Della shifted her weight. "There's something else, too. Take me. I know what folks have said. I'm as wild as a March wind and reckless and a little crazy. Johnny's the same, so the old gossips say we'll have the meanest kids in the country." She laughed softly. "Well, maybe we will. Right now I'm awful mad at Johnny, but I'll get over it. When he gets back from his stage run, we'll have a fight and I'll call him terrible names, but after that we'll make up and it will be wonderful. I love him, Kim. No matter what he does, I'll still love him. Don't ask me to explain why. I guess it's just the way a woman's heart works, and you can't explain that."

They rode on across the mesa, through the sage and the

scattered black dots that were the wind-shaped cedars, and
Kim's thoughts were as dark as the night that pressed down
around them. Della had been talking about her heart, but
she had been really trying to tell him about Rocky's.

Rocky must have loved him for a long time. When he had
needed help, she had been there. Kim Logan was not a pray-
ing man, but he prayed now, riding through the night with
the wind on his face and cold brilliant stars above him,
prayed that the knowledge of his love for Rocky had not
come too late.

They reached the pines, climbing steadily now, not far
north of the tableland where Kim and Yuma Bill had fought
Phil Martin and his bunch. Then, with dawn not more than
an hour away, they reached Abe Fawcett's place, windows
bright with lamplight.

"Keep your temper, Kim," Della said, "no matter what
happens. Maybe I made a mistake bringing you. I mean, Dad
and Ma and the rest of them up here have been afraid of
Clawhammer so long they're going to be hard to convince
about you."

"I know," he said, "but that ain't worrying me as much as
the time. It's gonna take all day to get 'em together."

"Dad started north when I left for town," she told him.
"They'll be at the Avis clearing a little before sunup."

As they reined up in front of the house, the front door
opened and Della's mother stood there, a rifle in her hands.
She called, "Who is it?"

"Me," Della answered. "Kim Logan's with me."

"Logan!" Mrs. Fawcett came down the path, Winchester
held on the ready. "You get out of here. Shorty Avis is lying
in my bed right now looking like he's going over the range,
and you've got the brass . . ."

"It wasn't Kim that done it," Della cut in. "Don't talk
like that. He's on our side."

"Our side," Mrs. Fawcett cried out in rage. "Maybe he
can pull the wool over your eyes, but he don't fool me. Not
a little bit. Now you get out of here, Logan, and . . ."

"Then I'll go, too," Della said quietly. "So will Rocky.
Doc here?"

"He's working on Shorty now. Don't get me sidetracked,
Della. We don't need this double-crossing gunslinger. If he's
on our side, which I doubt, he'll want pay and we haven't
got it to give him. I don't trust a man who fights for money,
and I wouldn't trust Kim Logan anyhow."

"You don't understand, Ma. There's been a lot that's happened the last few days. Everything's changed. Doc will tell
you that."

Mrs. Fawcett sniffed. "Everything's changed, has it? I'm

too old to swallow that. Nothing changes. You slap some paint on a tiger and you make him look different, but the stripes are still there. Same with a skunk."

Kim did not know Mrs. Fawcett as well as he knew Della and her father. Looking down at the woman now, he could not make out the expression on her face. It was just a pale blob topping a wide body, but her hostility was a tangible pressure laid against him. Della had said all she could, and Kim had a feeling that it would take very little to make Mrs. Fawcett fly into an insane rage and start shooting. If she did, no one on the mesa but Rocky and her own daughter would condemn her.

He had to work on her pride. It was the only weapon he could use, the same weapon he must use later when he faced Abe Fawcett and the rest of the mesa ranchers. He said evenly, "A skunk has his way of fighting, ma'am. But you take a band of sheep now. They're different. They just run."

He heard her gasp as if he'd knocked the wind out of her. She would give ground or she'd shoot. Pride was one of the few things these people had left. The younger ones like Rocky and Della did not remember, but the older ones, men and women both, would remember and they would be ashamed. Fear would be in them again when the time came that they must make the decision to fight or run, and all the tough talk in the world could not hide it.

Then he knew he had won, for she said harshly, "I suppose you think a skunk can protect sheep?"

"He can if he makes enough stink," he said.

Stepping down, Kim walked past Mrs. Fawcett and went into the house. A moment before she had been capable of shooting him in the back, but he was not afraid of that now. He heard the hum of talk between Della and her mother, then he was in the house and the sound of talk died.

The Fawcett house was a rambling, two-story structure built of logs, the most pretentious place on the mesa. The front room took up half of the lower floor. At one end an open stairway led to the bedrooms overhead; a cavernous stone fireplace occupied almost all of the other end. It was an inhospitable room, its furniture homemade and crude, the rough plank floor bare. Kim had never been here before, but now in this one quick glance, he had the feeling that the Fawcetts had hoped to hold a little of their past glory by building this huge house.

The kitchen formed one back quarter of the first floor, a bedroom the other quarter. The bedroom door was ajar, and Kim pushed it open and went in. Rocky stood at one side of the bed, Doc Frazee on the other. Shorty Avis lay motionless between them, a faded quilt pulled up under his chin. His head was bandaged, and his face was a mass of cuts and bruises.

Rocky turned, giving Kim a tired smile. Frazee rose and snapped his bag shut. "Nothing more I can do. He may come out of it. Can't tell yet. Just keep him quiet."

Frazee walked out. Kim crossed the room to stand beside Rocky, and looked down at Shorty's battered face. Shorty Avis was the one man on the mesa who would have stood and fought. That, Kim knew, was the reason he had been picked.

"I'm sorry," Kim said, realizing how utterly inadequate the words were.

He put an arm around Rocky. She turned and buried her face against his shirt. For a moment she stood that way, crying softly. It was the first time he had seen her break down, the first sign of weakness he had ever seen in her. She regained control of herself almost at once. She wiped a sleeve across her eyes and looked up at him, trying to smile.

"I didn't tell Della to let you know," she said, "but I'm glad she did. Thanks for coming."

"No need to thank me," he said.

He looked at Shorty's battered face, a slow anger beginning to burn in him. He had always considered himself a tough man, but this was too much. The way he saw it, a man under any circumstances had the right to a fair fight. They had not given Shorty Avis that, or any part of it.

"You see why I hate Peg Cody," Rocky breathed. "We knew this would happen after Dutch Heinz brought us that warning, but we didn't think it would be this soon."

He let the silence run on for a moment, making no effort to defend Peg. He said then, "If it hadn't been for me, you'd have been there."

"I've thought of that, Kim, but it wouldn't have made any difference. I couldn't have stopped them, and it might have been worse."

"I'm afraid it would," he said. "I'll square this, Rocky. That's a promise."

"Squaring it won't save Dad."

"It may save some others."

She moved away from him, her shoulders slack as if all the weariness and worry and fear that had crowded her for so long had finally caught up with her. "I know, Kim. It's got to be finished. We'll run or we'll fight, and if we fight, more men will die. It's wrong, it's all wrong."

"You said something about when the country grows up, men like me will disappear. I don't think so, Rocky. There'll always be things like this."

"Not if the law is strong," she whispered. "This wouldn't have happened if Ed Lane was a different man than he is."

Kim nodded, knowing it was true. He had seen this same drama played out time after time. Different names, different scenes, but essentially the same grim drama of strength bullying weakness. When law was only an ideal, a theory, people like Hank Dunning and Peg Cody, consumed by the fires of greed and ambition, could not be controlled, but the right kind of man wearing the star could make law something more than a theory.

It had always been that way; it always would be. The fault went back of Ed Lane, even back of Hank Dunning and Peg, back to the complacency of the people who permitted Lane's election. Brit Bonham and Doc Frazee as well as Fred Galt. And Kim Logan. He had not been here when Lane had been elected, but he had been in other places where the same thing had been done, and he had stood by, watching, and doing nothing.

"We'll get a different man," he said. "Now you'd better get some rest. You can't do anything for Shorty by standing here. It's out of your hands."

"Out of my hands," she breathed. "Yes, I guess it is."

She blew out the lamp and left the room, Kim following. Rocky went on into the kitchen. Doc Frazee had laid his black bag on the pine table in the middle of the room and had dropped into a rocking chair. Kim drew another chair up beside him and sat down, asking, "How bad is he, Doc?"

"Pretty damned bad," Frazee said gloomily. "Busted ribs. Concussion. A face that'll never look the same again." He shook his head. "They must have knocked him down and booted hell out of him. Pretty brave outfit, that bunch."

"I wouldn't call them that," Kim said.

Frazee gave him a straight look. "What are you going to do?"

"Why should I do anything?" Kim motioned toward the kitchen. Talk flowed through the open door. Mrs. Fawcett's voice rising above the girls, her tone bitter and accusing. "Della's ma don't believe I will."

Frazee stroked his goatee, bony face grave. He said finally, "I'll tell you. Some of us have our bets down on you, me and Brit and Rocky. Della, too, or she wouldn't have brought you out here. You gonna welsh on them bets?"

"I didn't make the bets," Kim said.

"Well, we made 'em for you. It adds up to the same thing."

"Looks to me like a thankless job. About like pulling a drowning man out of the river. He'll fight you like hell while you're saving him."

"Yeah, I know," Frazee said gloomily. "Same thing with me. Cuss me because I dose 'em with medicine that don't

121

taste good, but I keep on dosing 'em. Don't ask me why. I just do it."

Della came out of the kitchen. She said, "Breakfast is ready."

They ate by lamplight, Mrs. Fawcett plodding between the table and the big range to fill coffee cups or bring more biscuits and bacon. When they were done, a faint gray light had crept across the eastern sky.

Della said, "Time to ride, Kim. I'm going with you, but Rocky's staying with her pa."

Kim rose, nodding. Mrs. Fawcett stood with her back to the stove, a wide-hipped, shapeless woman, the mark of the hard years on her face and hands, on a body that might once have been as slim and attractive as her daughter's.

"Don't you get into none of the fighting, Della," Mrs. Fawcett said. "You come back here when the palaver's finished." Then she looked directly at Kim, doubt clouding her broad face. "We'll see how much stink a skunk can make, mister, and maybe you'll find out what a bunch of sheep can do."

"Then Hank Dunning and Dutch Heinz will be surprised," Kim said.

For just a moment Kim stood looking at Rocky, filling his eyes with the young vibrant beauty of her face. Then he wheeled and followed Della out of the house.

CHAPTER 17

BALL OF SAND

IT WAS full daylight when Kim and Della reached the clearing that only a few hours before had held the Avis buildings. Now there was nothing but the gray piles of ashes where the cabin and barn and other buildings had been. The cabin's chimney was still standing, a grim monument that would be here long after the ashes were scattered.

Kim had not wanted Della to come with him, but he knew that if he went alone, he would never convince the mesa ranchers of his intentions. Now, riding across the clearing, he saw that Della's presence was even more necessary than he had first thought.

Six men were hunkered in the yard, idly talking and smoking. The instant Kim was recognized, they stood up, hands dropping to gun butts. They began backing toward their horses, wary eyes on Kim. They would have started shooting before he'd ridden half the width of the clearing if Della had not been with him.

Della and Kim reined up ten paces from the men, Della smiling as if this were a pleasant social gathering. She motioned toward Kim, saying, "Boys, you know Kim Logan, don't you?"

"I'm sorry I do," one of them said. "What the hell you doing here, Logan?"

"I'm throwing in with you," Kim said. "You could use another gun."

They scowled, finding his words mentally indigestible. He stepped down, gave Della a hand, and swung away from the group. There would be enough explaining to do when the rest got here. He made a wide circle around the yard, leaving Della to talk to her neighbors. Presently two others rode in, and after ten minutes had passed, Abe Fawcett arrived with Clay Mackey. That was all. Kim joined the group then, standing beside Della and facing the others.

There was no talk for a time. Della had apparently said all that she could, and it hadn't been enough. They eyed him a moment, anger stirring in them. Then Fawcett said, "I've always had quite a bit of faith in Della's judgment in things like this, Logan, but I'm damned if I do this time. She says you want to throw in with us. Why?"

Kim stood motionless, his back held stiffly straight, probing blue eyes making a cool study of these men. Fawcett was as near a leader as there was among them. Big-chested and paunchy, Abe Fawcett had a pair of steel gray eyes and silver hair that gave him a sort of dignity, but his appearance would have been more impressive if he had not worn a sweeping mustache that added a faintly comical touch to a face that otherwise was quite severe.

Most of these men were, like Fawcett and Shorty Avis, middle-aged or older. Only two were young, sons who had stayed with their fathers. Most of the boys had drifted out of the country, knowing they weren't needed at home and that there was little chance of finding work in Ganado. The only possible jobs were with HD and Clawhammer. None of them wanted those jobs except Clay Mackey's three boys who were riding for Clawhammer.

"Well?" Fawcett prodded.

"I'll tell you why," Kim said, bringing his eyes to the big man. "We're on the same side. I can use some help and you can use another gun, so we'd be smart to team up."

Little Joe Scanlon, at the end of the line, shook his head. "It wouldn't be smart, mister. It'd be plain stupid. You've been riding around talking tough for Clawhammer. Been a year now. We've got no reason to think you've changed." He motioned around the clearing. "It's my guess you had a hand in this."

"You're guessing wrong, Joe," Kim said mildly. "A lot's happened the last three or four days. Everything's turned inside out. No use taking time to tell all of it, but there's two things you need to know. I couldn't have been here because Ed Lane had me in the jug on a murder that Phil Martin and Hank Dunning rigged. After I got out I was too busy keeping my neck out of a rope to be in on a torch party. The second thing is that Peg Cody fired me."

They were silent a moment, weighing his words in their minds. Then Fawcett said, "I ain't satisfied. You could pull us into a trap and get our heads shot off. We know you'd been warned to stay off Shorty's property." He motioned toward the chimney. "Might be your way of getting square with Shorty."

Kim shoved his thumbs into his belt, eyes moving along the line of hostile faces. "I'll tell you something else which I hadn't aimed to, but it's what makes the difference in me. I love Rocky."

They might have cursed him for wanting one of their women. Or laughed at him. They did neither. Instead they shifted uneasily, toes digging into the dirt, and he saw at once that he had said the one right thing.

Clay Mackey demanded, "You fixing to marry her and live up here?"

"I haven't asked her," Kim answered, "but I will if I'm alive when this is settled. If I live and Rocky will have me, we'll stay in the valley, but not here on the mesa. I don't think you boys will either. You'll be back on the creek where you belong."

Fawcett blew out a great breath, fat jowls trembling. "What kind of a damned fairy tale are you getting off?"

Kim smiled. "No fairy tale, Abe. Let me ask you a question. Why did you round these boys up?"

"Hell, you can see for yourself. I had a look at Shorty when Rocky fetched him in. I . . . why, damn it, Logan, I wanted the boys to see what Clawhammer will do if we don't stop 'em."

"How do you aim to stop Clawhammer?"

"Well, I . . . I thought we'd figure out something this morning."

Again Kim swung his gaze along the line of faces, not so hostile now, faces weathered by wind and sun, faces of men who wanted nothing but the right to live in peace and deeply frightened because they knew there was no peace for them.

"Then you need me," Kim said. "I know what to do."

Again they shifted uneasily, wanting his help but still uncertain about him. It was Della who said, "Don't stand there like a bunch of ninnies. Go on. Tell him we'll work with him."

"We could use some help," Fawcett said reluctantly, "but even if you're on the level, Logan, your gun won't make the difference. Dunning's outfit is at Clawhammer. We just ain't tough enough to lick 'em, and that's the truth."

"So you'll run again like you ran once before when Sam Cody kicked you off the creek," Kim said with biting contempt. "You don't really think you can win if you hang and rattle. You're wrong, Abe. I say you can."

"I reckon we'll go along with you," Joe Scanlon said. "Trouble is we allowed you'd be the one who did Peg Cody's pushing."

"Not me," Kim said. "Like everybody else, I figured she was scrapping with Dunning, but it don't look that way now. Anyhow, it's Dunning and Dutch Heinz who'll do the pushing, and they can be licked."

Kim hunkered in the dirt and picking up a stick, sketched a map of the valley. "My notion is to divide the valley. If others come in, we'll make room for 'em. As long as we can, anyhow. What I'm saying is that this can be a good cattle country for all of us. A lot of folks can make a living here without fighting and without making hogs out of ourselves."

He drew several lines across his map. "I ain't trying to tell you how to divide the valley, but it might work like this. Fawcett here." He made an F. "Scanlon here." He went on down the line, following the east side of the creek, filling in initials until he was finished. "It means buying good bulls and more cows. Putting up buildings and corrals. Going off and leaving what you've done here." He rose, facing them, and added, "Remember one thing. If you'd knocked Sam Cody's ears down a long time ago, you wouldn't be up here." He pointed at his map. "You'd be down there."

"Damn it to hell," Fawcett burst out. "This is worse than a fairy tale. We're trying to think of some way to save our homes, not move back to the creek and give Peg Cody a real excuse to wipe us out."

"You mean you wouldn't go back to the creek, Abe?" Kim asked. "That's funny. They tell me you used to be quite a cowman."

Fawcett got red in the face; his fat jowls were trembling again. He tried to say something and failed. Then Joe Scanlon said, "Even if we did move in on Clawhammer and made it stick, this would take money. We couldn't swing it, Logan."

"Brit Bonham's got money to loan," Kim said. "I talked to him about it yesterday. I claim that a lot of little outfits will bring more prosperity to this country than two big ones.

Brit will gamble, providing you boys will gamble your lives."

"We've got till sunset," Clay Mackey said worriedly.

"Maybe not that long. I'm guessing, but I figure Peg will leave her crew with the herd. It's Dunning's bunch we'll have to fight. Near as I can read the sign, there was nine or ten men here yesterday. That tallies with what Dunning's got." Kim pinned his eyes on Mackey. "If Peg was pulling her crew in, your boys would have been home before this, wouldn't they?"

"That's right," Mackey said, "if they knew what was up."

"I know the way Peg thinks," Kim went on. "It'll be cattle first and fight second. We lick Dunning and our troubles are over."

"Not if we're moving back on the creek." Scanlon pointed at the map. "That's Clawhammer range you're giving away."

"Clawhammer's done," Kim said. "Peg don't know it, but that's the way it is, providing we finish Dunning. The bank will close Peg out."

Fawcett shook his head doubtfully. "Don't make sense to me. Bonham won't close her out."

"He will. You'll see."

Fawcett swung to face his neighbors. "I wanted you boys to see this. Maybe it's Dunning or maybe it's Clawhammer, or both. Whichever way it is, you see what you're up against. Now we'd best get home. We'll keep our eyes open and . . ."

"No," Kim said.

Fawcett wheeled to face him. "You ain't giving the orders."

"I am if I'm with you in this ruckus."

"He said he knew what to do," Scanlon said.

"All right," Fawcett muttered reluctantly. "If you've got a plan, let's hear it."

"Fighting's an old game to me," Kim said, "but a blind man could see it's new to you. If you go back to your homes, you're licked. Dunning will knock you off one at a time. The only chance you've got is to stick together and take the fight to them. If you want your women safe, let Della fetch 'em to her place."

"There wouldn't be nobody there to fight . . ." Fawcett began.

"I've got a hunch your women will put up quite a scrap. Now I'll tell you what I want you to do. Give me half an hour's start. Then you light out for Clawhammer, but don't go on down. Leave your horses on the bench, back a piece so they won't be seen from the house. Then you wait there. Keep watching. About noon or later Dunning and his boys will ride out. Let 'em get close before you give it to 'em. Surprise has won more fights than hot lead, and they'll sure be surprised."

126

"We'll be leaving our homes wide open," Scanlon objected.

"They'll be wide open if you all go home and figure on fighting by yourselves. That's what they'll expect. Dunning knows you boys ran once when Sam Cody wanted your places. He'll figure on your running again."

They looked at each other, bitter men, shamed by their past record, held here now only by their pride. Watching them, Kim could not be sure what the end would be. Welding them into a fighting unit was about as difficult as making a ball of dry sand.

"All right," Clay Mackey said at last. "We'll be there."

Kim mounted his horse.

"Where are you going?" Fawcett demanded.

"To Clawhammer."

"You can't, Kim," Della cried. "They'll kill you."

"Maybe," Kim agreed, "but I'm figuring on surprise being on my side. Anyhow, there's a thing or two I need to know."

"And something they'll need to know," Scanlon shouted. "You can tell 'em where we'll be."

"I could." Kim turned to his buckskin and stepped up. He sat his saddle, eyes searching their faces, worried and uncertain. He said, "I may need some help if it don't go like I figure."

"If Rocky was here, she wouldn't let you do this," Della said.

Leaning down, he said in a low tone, "I've never told Rocky I love her. If I don't see her again, I'd like for her to know." Reining his horse around, he rode across the clearing and into the timber.

CHAPTER 18

IN THE LION'S MOUTH

IT WAS well toward noon when Kim reached the bench above Clawhammer and looked down upon the big house and barns and maze of corrals. Sam Cody had built well, certain of his future and equally certain that he had trained Peg to run the ranch as efficiently as he had. But there are always two uncertain factors over which a cowman has little control, weather and the price of beef. They had combined to beat bigger men than Sam Cody, and they had beaten him.

The early trouble in the valley was ancient history. Kim had never heard the whole story, but he knew enough. History never fully died; fingers of the past continually reach into the future, and it was that way with Clawhammer. Peg had inherited Sam Cody's ambition and lax ethics, so she was using the same ruthless, pushing tactics he had used.

Kim, sitting his saddle at the edge of the bench, found the same questions prodding his mind that had been there for hours. How much had Peg ever really counted on him? Had she turned fully to Dutch Heinz? Had she gone to Dunning or had Dunning come to her? That was the difference between her and her father. She was forced to look to men to help carry out her plans, Sam had needed no one.

Still, the answers to these questions were not important, not when Kim thought of Yuma Bill, of Shorty Avis and the ashes that had been his and Rocky's home. If the chance came, Kim would kill Hank Dunning as quickly as he would kill any wild animal that needed killing. He would do the same to Dutch Heinz. But it was different with Peg. In that way her woman's weakness was her strength. He could not beat her down with his fists: he could not draw a gun on her. Even the law would not touch her unless the evidence against her was conclusive. So far it was not.

Kim rode down off the bench and crossed the creek. He could not make a definite plan of action until he saw the shape of things. There were those who would have said he was crazy for coming in like this, but it seemed worth the risk. Regardless of the part Peg had in the trouble, Hank Dunning was the hub around which it revolved. If Dunning was dead, trouble would disintegrate like a whirling wheel coming apart, and a dozen lives would be saved. It was a gamble, Kim Logan's life balanced against those that might be saved.

There was a knot of men in front of the barn. Dunning's riders, Kim saw as he came up, but Dunning wasn't with them. They were covertly watching Kim while appearing to be idling there. Limpy was not in sight. Neither was Dutch Heinz.

It was as peaceful a scene as a man would find, too peaceful, and Kim was warned by the very innocence of it. He reined up and dismounted, keeping the buckskin between him and the men by the barn. While he tied, his eyes swept the yard. Apparently no one else was around. He stepped away from the hitch pole and deliberately rolled a smoke, standing so that Dunning's men could see him.

The thing was wrong. It was too casual, so casual that it must have been carefully planned to appear this way. Kim felt a chill ravel down his spine as he considered the two things he could do. He could walk straight toward Dunning's crew with his gun in his hand, or he could ignore them and go into the house. Dunning was probably inside, and because Dunning was the man he wanted, he chose the house. It was too late to back out now. He had to play it through.

He fired his cigarette and flipped the match away, then turned up the path to the house. The front door was open. No one was in sight in the big living room. He stepped up on the porch, throwing a quick glance at the men in front of the barn. They were openly watching him now, tense. He went on across the porch, hand on gun butt. If he read the sign right, this was trouble.

Kim stepped through the door. He had no chance to pull his gun. Dutch Heinz was waiting for him, back pressed against the wall. He slammed into Kim, big fist battering him in the stomach. It was treacherous and unexpected, a brutal blow that slammed wind out of him and sent him reeling back through the door. He had a brief glimpse of Peg and Dunning behind Heinz; he heard a yell from the men at the barn and the pound of boots as they ran toward the house.

Heinz had a slow stubborn mind, the sort that never forgave an old injury. Now the need to square accounts with Kim made a driving maniac out of him. He hammered Kim with one fist and then the other, in the stomach, on the chest, on the head. Kim had been caught off balance and kept that way; he had no chance to swing an effective fist. He backed across the porch, trying to block Heinz's blows, to hold long enough to gain the initiative, but it was like trying to dam a stream in high flood.

Kim fell backward off the porch. He landed on his back and yanked his gun clear of leather. Heinz was poised on the edge of the porch, instinctively planning to jump on him, but he held himself there, teetering and swearing in a tough wicked voice. Kim lay motionless, gun tilted up to cover Heinz, while he fought to drag breath into aching lungs.

Dunning's men were there then, but they didn't close in, for the first move would have brought death to Heinz. Slowly Kim came to his feet. He said, "You've got an iron, Dutch. I'm putting mine back. Then we'll settle this."

Heinz shook his head. "Not me. I heard about Tonto Miles." He motioned to Dunning's men. "You're done, Logan. Too many of us. What'n hell did you ride in here for?"

"I didn't expect this." Kim backed away now so that he could watch Heinz and Dunning's crew. "I thought you'd be out of the country. Ed Lane's looking for you."

Heinz laughed jeeringly. "Not now he ain't. He was out here this morning, but he decided he didn't want to be sheriff no more. He's halfway to Del Norte by now."

"He resigned?"

"Resigned? Hell, he quit. We don't have no sheriff at all now, not any."

Dunning had crossed the porch to stand beside Heinz, towering above him, his black hair rebellious and uncombed. A smile touched the corners of his long-lipped mouth; his dark eyes seemed entirely lacking in expression. Somehow Dunning was able to clothe himself with a sort of arrogant dignity. It was that dignity which had given him the reputation he had in the valley.

"Why are you here, Logan?" Dunning asked.

"Natural enough for me to be here," Kim answered. "But it ain't for you. Or maybe you're taking Clawhammer over."

Dunning shrugged. "Now maybe I am. Or put it the other way. Clawhammer's taking HD over. I want to know why you're here."

"I want to see Peg."

Dunning jerked his head at the door. "Put your gun up. She's inside."

"I'll keep my gun in my fist. I'm not giving my back to your wolf pack."

"Drop your gun, Kim," Peg called. "You'll have a chance to see me, but not with a gun in your hand."

She was behind him. She must have gone out through the back door and come around the house. He made a slow turn; he saw the Winchester in her hands. He had no doubt she would use it, for she was very close now to the thing she had been working for.

"Looks like your pot," Kim said, and shoved his gun into holster.

That was when Heinz came off the porch in a headlong rush. Kim whirled and sidestepped and swung a fist to Heinz's face as he charged by. Then the roof fell on Kim. Dunning's crew swarmed over him and he went down. He struck out, squirmed and kicked, tried to roll, to break free, to get space in which to fight, but there were too many. They smothered him by sheer weight, but even then, with consciousness almost battered out of him, he heard Peg's voice, "Quit it. That's enough. Damn you, I said it was enough."

Kim lay on his back, winded and hurt, staring up at men who seemed to be ten feet tall. They had backed away, and Peg was standing over Kim, her cocked Winchester held on the ready. "Hank, maybe it was a good thing this happened. Now get this through your head. Marrying me won't make any difference about one thing. I'm giving the orders on Clawhammer and I'll keep on giving them."

"You're forgetting Chuck Dale," Dunning said in a low bitter voice. "He's the boy I lost off the rim the day Logan brought Yuma Bill here. You're forgetting Tonto Miles and

Pat Monroney. And you're forgetting you said Logan was just a drifter you could get rid of any time you wanted to. He's blocked everything we've tried from the minute he took Yuma Bill off the stage, and I aim to stop it."

"I'm not going to stand here and let your boys kick him to death," Peg snapped. "Not after I told him he'd have a chance to see me."

"He's been damned hard to kill," Dunning said in the same bitter tone. "We'd best do the job while we've got his fangs pulled."

"He'll wait," Peg said. "Your boys have got a job to do. Get them started on it."

"Not time yet," Dunning said.

For a moment they stood facing each other, straight-backed and proud, their wills clashing. Then Dunning broke under the force of Peg's stare, and turning, motioned his men back to the barn.

Heinz remained by the steps, great shoulders hunched forward in the ape-like posture that was characteristic of him. He said, "You've made some mistakes before, Peg, but saving this hombre's hide is the biggest one. You're soft."

"Soft?" Peg shook her head. "Not me, Dutch. I just think a little farther than you do. Kim may be some good to us alive, but he's no good to anybody if he's dead." She prodded Kim with a toe. "Get up. I'm locking you in the storeroom."

Kim got to his feet, reeling a little as he wiped a sleeve across his battered face. Peg pulled his gun. He stood staring at her, his vision clearing. She was wearing riding clothes; her red hair was carelessly pinned on the back of her head, and her hazel eyes that he had so often seen filled with good humor were sharp and calculating.

Turning, Kim walked past the glowering Heinz and into the house. He went on through the kitchen and into the store-room behind it, stumbling occasionally, for he was still groggy from the beating he had taken. He dropped down on a sack of sugar and held his head, a steady pain flashing across his temples.

Peg stood in the doorway a moment, looking at him. She said, "I wish you hadn't come here, Kim, I wish you hadn't." She stepped back and, closing the door, twisted the turnpin. There had been a note of sincere regret in her voice as if she had been talking to a man condemned to death.

CHAPTER 19

ALL BETS ARE DOWN

KIM LOGAN had never been one to doubt his own destiny, but there were doubts in his mind now. He was in a tighter spot than when Ed Lane had locked him up in the Ganado jail. He'd had a few friends in town, but here he had none.

He walked around the room that was filled with the composite food smells of Clawhammer's supplies. Sam Cody must have planned it for a jail. There were only two windows, both high and so small that a grown man could not have escaped through either of them. The door was at the other end of the room. Kim had often noticed it when there had been no thought in his mind that some day he would be held behind it, and he had wondered why a mere storeroom needed a door so thick and so solidly hinged.

Kim put a shoulder against the door and pushed. There was no give to it. He stepped away and slammed against it and bounced back. No use. Tactics like that would get him nothing but a sprained shoulder. Kim, always a realist, had no illusions about his position. It was practically hopeless. He didn't know why Peg had saved his life, but he was sure of one thing. Sooner or later Dunning and Heinz would wear her down, and they'd have their way with him.

It must have been close to an hour after Kim had been locked in the storeroom that the door swung open. Limpy came in with a plate of food and a steaming cup of coffee. Peg stood behind him in the doorway with her Winchester. She said, "I'm going to town this afternoon and I didn't want you to get hungry."

Limpy set the plate and cup down on a box of condensed milk. He said, "You sure played hell coming back, Logan. Why didn't you have sense enough to stay away?"

"I didn't figure Peg meant it when she said I was fired," Kim answered.

Peg waited until Limpy left the storeroom. Then she said, "Don't try to jump me. Hank and Dutch want to see you dead. I don't."

"Maybe you mean you don't want the job of beefing me. You can always hire somebody to do dirty jobs like that."

Two spots of red showed on her cheeks, but she held her temper. "No, I don't mean that. I don't want you killed, but

I don't know what to do with you." She made a gesture with a hand as if begging him to believe her. "I've done some things I'm ashamed of because I've been a little crazy with my dreams about Clawhammer, but I haven't knowingly been guilty of murder. Please believe that."

"Maybe you think Yuma Bill died of measles."

"No. Dutch shot him, but not because I ordered it. I told him to take the money, but like a fool, he didn't wear a mask, so he killed the old man to shut his mouth."

Peg was silent a moment while she watched Kim eat. Then she asked, "Why did you really come here?"

"To get Dunning. That's what you hired me for."

"What made you think you'd find him here?"

"Rocky said you and him were working together. She says you're in love with him."

"You don't believe that," she flared.

"I'm wondering."

"Clawhammer's the only thing I love. You ought to know that by now."

"So you're marrying Dunning because you love Clawhammer. Now that makes a lot of sense."

"Of course it does. After I marry Hank there won't be any HD. Just Clawhammer range on both sides of the creek."

"Think you can run Dunning?"

"Of course. I never saw a man I couldn't run. Except you." She shook her head. "Kim, I'm sorry the way it's gone between us, but I gave you every chance that night and you wouldn't take it."

"You'd already promised Dunning, hadn't you?"

She shrugged. "A promise doesn't mean much to me. I aimed to buy the best husband for Clawhammer I could get. I thought for a while you'd be the one, but that night I found out you had too many fool notions about the mesa ranchers."

"Clawhammer's got along without the mesa range."

"It won't. Not with the plans I have. Anyhow, you're too soft. Or maybe it was because you're in love with Rocky Avis. Anyhow, I found out you wouldn't do."

"No, I reckon I wouldn't, but nobody ever said I was soft before. Looks to me like you've got some pretty big schemes cooked up for Clawhammer, or you wouldn't want the mesa range so bad."

She nodded, letting him see the satisfaction that was in her. "I have. I'm not patient, Kim, and I won't grow old waiting to do what I want to do. Clawhammer will be the biggest outfit in the state. Maybe in the nation. I'll have the valley and the mesa and the high range to boot. All mine just like I told you that night."

"The little fry won't run, Peg. You're spreading too far. You've fixed it so you've got to win or you're finished."

She laughed scornfully. "I will win, and you're loco about the little fry. They'll run all right. Dad's mistake was in not chasing them across the divide when he moved them off the creek."

"You're wrong, Peg. Why can't you hang onto what you've got and be satisfied."

"I wasn't born to be satisfied. I know people, so I don't have the slightest doubt about the way this will go. When a man has run once he'll run again. That's why I'm going to town this afternoon. They'll be there to sell to me."

"You gave the order to bust Shorty Avis up?"

She nodded. "I had to show them what would happen if they had any notion of fighting. Before I'm done, I'll have the little fry off the other side of the valley, too."

Kim finished his meal, thinking he had heard the truth from Peg at last. She was a greedy fool reaching for everything when most people would have been satisfied with what she had. She had been carried away by the magnificence of her dreams, she was counting on Hank Dunning and Dutch Heinz, and in the end she would destroy herself.

"Funny thing," he said. "I guess I know you better than anyone in the valley."

She laughed lightly. "Of course you do. I still wish you were on my side, but it's too late now." Her face turned grave then. "You're like the rest of them, Kim, a sucker for a kiss, but you insist on still being a man, and that's the reason I knew I couldn't manage you." She motioned toward the rear wall. "Step back and I'll get your plate and cup. I've got to ride."

He moved back, asking, "Why did you hire me in the first place and put out this fake war talk?"

"Money. That's the whole answer. I wanted a lot of money to stock Clawhammer range, so I borrowed thirty thousand from Bonham. I got his sympathy by telling him Dunning would push me off the range if I didn't hold it. Of course I didn't want him or anyone else to know that Dunning was going to work up a rush on his bank so we could buy my notes back. It would have worked if you hadn't delivered Yuma Bill's money."

Peg picked up Kim's plate and cup and moved back to the door, smiling ruefully. "As for hiring you, I had to make some show of protecting myself against Hank. You rode in just when I was looking for a tough hand and you looked like one. At the time I didn't realize you really were a tough hand." She stood there a moment looking at him, frowning.

134

"Maybe I'll figure out what to do with you while I'm gone. I just wish you'd ridden off like I told you to."

He said nothing while she moved out of the storeroom, her Winchester covering him until the door swung shut. It was clear enough now. Bonham had fallen into Peg's trap when he'd loaned her the thirty thousand, and the fake war had accomplished exactly what Peg had wanted it to. She was a woman pretending to hold out against a ruthless neighbor, and because she was a woman, she had succeeded in winning sympathy, something old Sam Cody had never done. In her way she was a genius, a great actress hiding her real ambition from Brit Bonham and Doc Frazee and the rest of the townsmen.

Thirty thousand dollars for ten! That was how her deal with Bonham had been meant to work. Dunning had been in Bonham's office that morning trying to buy Peg's notes and Bonham had come very close to making the deal. Kim laughed, a sour laugh, for it was a sour kind of joke, this sympathy they'd had for Peg while she had been planning a neat profit of twenty thousand.

It hadn't worked, but still Peg was talking about having the biggest outfit in the state or even in the nation. Wild talk, the crazy talk of a woman consumed by her ambition. Crazy or not, she was coldly logical. It meant, then, that she had another idea to make quick money, a lot of money, for her grandiose plans would not include any penny-ante business.

A sense of futility touched Kim. This thing still had to be fought to its final irrevocable end. Dunning and Dutch Heinz had to die, and Peg would have to leave the valley, but here he was, a prisoner without any kind of a weapon. The chances were good that while Peg was gone, Heinz would come in and shoot him.

Thinking about it now, Kim realized that for all of Peg's expressed love for Clawhammer and her wild dreams about it, there was a real difference between her and Dutch Heinz and Dunning. She had a soft spot whether she would admit it or not, Heinz and Dunning did not. She had saved his life today. By that one act she had showed that the gulf between her and these men she thought she was using was wide and deep.

There was no sense in sitting here and waiting for Heinz to come in and finish him. He began searching the room for some kind of a weapon, any kind that would give him a chance. There was nothing. Not even an ax handle. Then, in desperation, he kicked a flour barrel apart, coughing as a white cloud swirled up around his head. He picked up a stave, balanced it in his hand, and shook his head. A sorry weapon, but the best he could find.

135

He walked to the door, shoved some boxes out of the corner, and moved into it, putting his back against the wall. Somebody would come after him, probably Heinz, and if he didn't see Kim, it would be natural enough to step inside. The barrel stave, brought down in a sharp blow across a man's wrist, would make him drop a gun. Then Kim would have a chance, for the blow would be painful and there would probably be a moment of shocked surprise that would give Kim an opportunity to beat him to the dropped gun.

The big house must have been deserted, for no sound came from it as the minutes dragged by. Then another hope came to Kim. Perhaps Dunning and Heinz had ridden out. They might not return until after Peg did. Still, it was a thin hope. She had saved his life once; it was doubtful if she could do it again.

Suddenly Kim was aware of gunfire. He ran to a window and looked out, but he could not see anyone. The shooting came from the north, and he could see nothing but the bench which lay directly behind the house. He turned back to the door, anxiety growing in him. He guessed what had happened. The mesa ranchers had waited on the other side of the creek, and when Dunning and his bunch had left Clawhammer, they'd ridden into an unexpected fight.

The firing grew closer. Then Kim heard steps on the kitchen floor. He drew back into his corner, raising the stave. The door was pulled open, and Limpy called, "Logan! Logan! Where the hell are you?"

Kim's hands tightened on the stave, nerves tense, but Limpy did not come in. He remained in the kitchen just outside the door, and he cried out again, his voice frantic. "Logan, here's your gun. No sense hiding this way. I don't like Dunning's bunch no better than you do."

Kim didn't understand, but this was no time to wonder why Limpy was doing this. The shooting was close now, almost in front of the house. Kim lunged through the door, slamming Limpy down and knocking the gun out of his hand.

"What'd you do that for?" the old man yelled. "Hell, I was just trying to help . . ."

Kim scooped up the gun. "I didn't know whether you were alone or not."

"Nobody else around here who'd give you a hand," Limpy cried. "I can see through that damned horse thief of a Dunning if Peg can't. I kept telling her she had no business letting him come around here. She can't make no silk purse out of a sow's ear. She should have taken a shotgun to Dunning the first time . . ."

But Kim wasn't waiting to hear the old man. He checked the gun and ran out of the kitchen and through the living

136

room and on to the porch. The fight was directly in front of the house. It was the last thing Kim expected. The mesa ranchers had got the jump on Dunning's riders and had chased them back across the creek.

For a moment there seemed to be no pattern to the fight. The yard was filled with milling horses, smoke made a swirling fog over them, guns roared, and men shouted and bawled out wild oaths and cried shrilly in agony. Kim stepped down off the porch, thinking that this would be the end, one way or the other, that it could be fought out to a final bloody end here in Clawhammer's yard.

Dutch Heinz' great voice bawled out an order above the uproar, "Inside. Inside." Kim saw Heinz come off his horse and plunge toward the house, some of Dunning's crew following.

Then Heinz saw Kim and he stopped flat-footed, a strangled involuntary cry coming out of him. Kim sensed the fear that was in the man; he had this one quick look at the wide-jawed face. Heinz had his gun in his hand. He came on now, lifting his .45 and throwing a shot at Kim that came too late, for Kim had laced a bullet into his great chest.

Heinz rocked forward and fell, hands flung out, and lay still. Kim stepped over him and went on. He felt the sting of a slug gouging flesh away from a rib; he fired again and knocked another man off his feet. Limpy, on the porch behind Kim, let go with a shotgun, the load of buckshot blowing a huge hole in a man's stomach.

It was enough. Caught between Kim's and Limpy's fire on one side and that of the mesa ranchers' on the other, the rest of Dunning's outfit threw up their hands. Kim called out, "Hold it. Hold it."

There were four of them still on their feet, two wounded and two untouched by bullets but badly scared and having all desire for fighting knocked out of them. Kim kept them covered until Abe Fawcett tramped up, his neighbors strung out behind him, some bleeding from bullet wounds and all filled with the glow of complete and unexpected victory.

"Where's Dunning?" Kim demanded.

Fawcett stopped, surprised as if he had not thought of Dunning, and stared at the dead men on the ground. He said, "Why, I never saw Dunning. Maybe he wasn't with 'em."

"He wasn't," Joe Scanlon said. "I'll swear to it, Logan. Heinz was running the outfit. They rode right into us. Didn't figure we were within ten miles of here. It was like you said. Surprise was worth a couple of cannons. We knocked hell out of 'em with the first volley. They lit out for here and we got on their tails as soon as we could hit leather."

Kim motioned to Fawcett. "Take these hombres inside.

137

Patch 'em. Looks like some of your boys need a little patching, too." He swung to face Limpy. "Where's Dunning?"

Limpy threw a scared look at the mesa men. "Kim, you tell these hombres I helped you. Tell em I didn't like Dunning and Heinz, neither."

"All right, all right," Kim said hurriedly. "Hear that, Abe? Limpy's on our side. Treat him right."

"You bet," Fawcett said. "I seen what he done with that scatter-gun."

"Where's Dunning?" Kim asked again.

But Limpy was not to be hurried. "What about Peg? This ain't her fault. It was Dunning's and Heinz's."

"I want to know where Dunning is," Kim shouted in exasperation. "What's the matter with you?"

Limpy gripped his shotgun with white-knuckled hands, harried eyes swinging around the half circle of men in front of him. "He's in town. Rode in with Peg. I want to know about her. I promised Sam the day he died that I'd look out for her. I tried to keep her out of this, but she was too damned stubborn to listen. You can't hang a woman. What about her, Kim?"

"She's got to leave the valley," Kim said. "If she don't try to make more trouble, she won't be hurt. That's the only promise I can make."

Limpy licked dry lips, trembling now as he pinned his gaze on Kim. "Dunning aimed to show up in town and tell folks that him and Peg had buried the hatchet. No more trouble. Then about dusk he was gonna leave. These fellers was supposed to run everybody off the mesa this afternoon and they'd swear Dunning was with 'em all night. Then after dark he was going back to town to rob the bank. He was gonna take all the cash and get Peg's notes."

Then it wasn't over. It wouldn't be over until Hank Dunning was dead. Kim put a hand to his side where the bullet had raked a rib. He threw his hand away and stared blankly at the blood, trying to think what was to be done.

Scanlon shouted, "Let's go get Dunning and hang him."

"I'll get him," Kim said. "I'll send Doc out. Take care of your wounded. I'll fetch Heinz's body with me so Dunning will see how it is. You can bring the rest in later."

"You'll need help," Scanlon said.

Kim shook his head. "No. This is my job. I'll do it. Alone."

CHAPTER 20

DUST TO DUST

IT WAS late afternoon when Kim reached the fringe of cabins that surrounded Ganado. He was leading Heinz's horse, the dead man lashed face-down across the saddle. All the way in from Clawhammer he had thought about Peg. She had saved his life today. He would probably never know exactly what her motive had been, but regardless of motive, the fact that she had saved his life could not be questioned. Whatever she had done and planned to do, he owed a debt to her.

Before Kim had left Clawhammer, Limpy had drawn him aside, saying, "Peg just couldn't look ahead. That was her whole trouble. She ain't bad. She was just mixed up about what she could make men do. Dunning wanted to marry her all right, but then there wouldn't have been no Clawhammer. Just HD. Heinz knew that, but Dunning was paying him on the side, unbeknownst to Peg. All them shenanigans like busting Bonham and getting Peg's notes cheap was Dunning's ideas. If Sam had lived, he'd have busted Dunning sooner or later, but after Sam cashed in, Dunning set to work on Peg, telling her how they'd have the biggest outfit in the valley, chase the little fellers out and put more cows on this range than there is in the state of Texas. She took it all in, bait, hook, and sinker."

Limpy had gripped Kim's arm then. "I tell you she ain't bad, boy. Young and foolish and full of big wild ideas. That's all. She just didn't see all the misery she was bringing on the valley. Take care of her, will you?"

There was nothing for Kim to say except to repeat, "She'll have to leave the valley. She won't be hurt if she does."

"Then I'll go with her," Limpy said. "Tell her that."

Now, with Ganado before him, Kim did not know what to say to Peg, or what he could make her do. His thoughts were on her rather than Dunning, for there was no doubt of Dunning's part in this trouble but there was of Peg's. She was stubborn and she was proud, and she would not easily give up the fine dreams that had been hers.

He remembered his talk with her the night he had brought Yuma Bill to Clawhammer. She had said she'd stayed awake at nights, dreaming about what she was going to do and thinking of the mistakes her father had made. She wouldn't

139

make them; she would use the weapons the Lord gave a woman. That had been her mistake. Now, thinking about her and about old Sam Cody, it struck Kim that it was Sam who was really to blame for what Peg had done. He had died, plagued by a sense of failure, and Peg, possessed of the same big plans that had been in her father's mind, had been driven by an obsession to carry those plans to fulfillment.

Kim rode down Main Street, watching for Dunning and Peg, and seeing neither of them. He reined up and dismounted. Someone saw him and raised a cry. Kim waited while men crowded around him, Bonham and Doc Frazee and Johnny Naylor and half a dozen more, all throwing questions at him.

Kim handed Bonham a heavy money belt. "I reckon that's Yuma Bill's. I took it off Heinz." He told them what had happened. Then he sensed that something was wrong and stopped talking.

Bonham said softly, "There's Dunning."

Men spilled away as Kim made a slow turn. Dunning stood in front of the hotel, bare-headed, black hair freshly trimmed and slicked down. Peg was behind him in the lobby, staring through a window, and at this distance Kim could not see the expression that was on her face. But there was no mistaking Dunning's.

The HD owner must have been surprised to see Kim; he must have been more surprised when he saw Heinz's body. But there was more than surprise on his eagle-beaked face. There was a cold and bitter hatred for this man whom he had regarded too lightly. His long lips were pulled so tightly against his teeth that they made a thin bitter line; he still wore his cloak of arrogant dignity, but the air of cool assurance that was usually a part of him was gone. Kim thought, *He can't duck a fight now and he knows it.*

Kim stood motionless a few feet in front of the horse that carried Heinz's body, the slanting sunlight hard upon him, his shadow a long dark streak at his side. He was remembering Tonto Miles and his own thoughts when he had fought Miles. He had been forced to kill the man to get at Dunning. Now the moment was here.

The seconds ticked by; the town was very quiet, waiting. Still Dunning stood there, tall, his hawk-nosed face mirroring the cold rage that gripped him. Then Kim laid his voice against the man, "Your string's wound up, Dunning. The mesa bunch was waiting for your outfit and shot hell out of 'em."

Dunning stepped down off the walk, hand within inches of gun butt, black eyes on Kim as he took two deliberate steps. There was a chance for him even at this time if he

140

could outdraw Kim, for the valley people had long been in the habit of obeying him, and such a habit would be hard to break as long as he could beat down those who had the courage to stand against him.

Two deliberate steps. That was all, then his hand moved toward gun butt, very fast, and the barrel was clear of leather and coming up. Two shots rolled out together, the reports hammering against the false front of Ganado's Main Street, hammered out and were thrown back, and faded. Two shots, no more. Kim stood motionless, smoke curling up from the muzzle of his .44, and waited until Dunning's knees gave and he spilled forward and the slanting sunlight fell across his back.

Someone yelled from the front of the drugstore, a high yell that was almost a scream. Another gun sounded from the boardwalk behind Kim and to his right. He whirled, his .44 coming up. Then he lowered it. It was Johnny Naylor who had fired. He held his Colt in front of him, eyes fixed on the drugstore. Kim, turning to look, saw Phil Martin, clad only in his underwear, fall forward out of the doorway. Then Kim knew what had happened. Martin, dog-like in his devotion, had made this futile effort to square accounts for Hank Dunning.

"Thanks, Johnny," Kim said. "I didn't expect that from you."

Naylor gave him a tight grin. "Della's been currying me with her tongue ever since the stage got in. You're all right, Logan. She pounded that into me."

Kim slipped his gun into holster and walked across the street to the hotel. He stepped into the lobby. Peg stood motionless at the window. She said without turning, "Looks like I put my money on the wrong man."

"The wrong man," he said, and walked to her. "Now you're finished."

"You haven't touched Clawhammer," she said.

"Bonham will do that. The biggest mistake you made was to think that because a man ran once he'd run again." He told her what had happened at Clawhammer, and added. "You've got one chance to get out of here with a little money in your pocket. Go see Brit. Sell for anything he'll give you. Otherwise he'll close you out and you'll have nothing."

Bonham will do that. The biggest mistake you made was to think that because a man ran once he'd run again." He "I'm remembering you saved my life this morning, Peg. I'd like to do more for you, but I can't. You'll have to leave the valley."

Dunning's and Heinz's bodies had been moved from the street, but men still stood in little groups talking about what had happened. She made a slow turn from the window and looked at Kim, her face softening. She asked, "Why do you want to help me?"

"I told you," he answered. "You saved my life."

"That all?"

There was more, much more, but he had no words to tell her about this fault of his, this loyalty to Clawhammer that had been as misplaced as her faith in Dutch Heinz had been. But it was not a question of loyalty now. If she stayed, there would be more trouble. There had been enough.

He said, "That's all. You haven't got a friend in the valley but Limpy. He said to tell you he'll go with you."

"Not a friend in the valley," she said as if talking to herself. "I'm Sam Cody's girl. I guess that's the whole trouble. He never tried to make friends. I have, but now there's just Limpy." She put her hands behind her back, fingers laced together, eyes pinned on his lean face. "You've been right about a lot of things, Kim, and I've been wrong. I guess you're right about this. I'll see Bonham and I'll ride out of the valley with Limpy."

If she felt any grief over Dunning's and Heinz's deaths, she gave no indication of it. She moved past him and left the hotel, her shoulders square, her back very straight, her face rigid, hiding any emotion that was in her.

Kim could not hate her, even when he thought of Yuma Bill. She had gambled everything, utterly ignoring all rules, and now she had lost everything that was important to her. She was to be pitied. It was a word he had never thought he would apply to Peg Cody. He knew that she was not escaping her punishment; she would never be free from the hell of her thoughts, the regret that came from failure.

Kim waited until Peg disappeared into the bank, then he walked to the drugstore. Doc Frazee stood in front with Luke Haines and Fred Galt. Kim said, "There's some men at Clawhammer who need you."

"I'll go out right away," Frazee said.

"Peg will be out for her things. Tell Fawcett and the rest of 'em that she's leaving the valley."

"I'll tell 'em." Frazee cleared his throat. "I've been waiting to talk to you before I went out there, Kim. Maybe you heard that Ed Lane had a stomachful of being sheriff and lit a shuck out of the country. How would you like the star?"

"I never packed a star in my life," Kim said.

"We ain't worried about how you'll make out," Frazee said quickly, and even Fred Galt nodded agreement. "We need a good man, now that we've got a new deal for the valley."

"Let me think about it, Doc," Kim said. "Right now I've got a ride to make."

Frazee grinned and winked. "Sure. And Shorty's gonna be all right. He came around before I left Fawcett's."

Turning, Kim strode to his horse and mounted, glad to hear that Shorty Avis would make it, for he had been afraid that Avis had been too badly injured to live. He rode out of town to the east, suddenly filled with a driving urgency to see Rocky, and his thoughts were filled with the things he must say to her.

Hours later he reached the Fawcett place. The door was open; he saw Rocky's slim figure in the rectangle of light and he forgot the words he had planned to say.

She ran to him, crying, "Kim, Kim," and he came down off his horse in a quick swinging motion and opened his arms to her. She was in them then, saying again, "Kim, Kim," and he found her hungry lips. It was like no other kiss, and he knew what Yuma Bill had meant when he had said there were some things which lasted and a man had to find them for himself.

She drew back, and looked up at him, her hands cupped against his cheeks, and he remembered some of the things he had planned to say. "I love you," he said. "I never knew what love was before, but I've learned from you."

"I knew how I felt about you," she said simply, "and I kept hoping that sometime you'd feel the same way about me."

"But I was twins. You were loving the man you wanted me to be."

She laughed softly. "I was loving the man you were, the real Kim Logan. You just had to find out for yourself. When you came back, I knew you'd found out."

"I reckon you'd call that faith," he said. "You were right about something else, too. About me being a snake stomper and not a brush popper. I kept telling myself I wanted a ranch, but seems like it's kind of hard to get away from stomping snakes. They asked me to be sheriff, but if you . . ."

"No, Kim. It's what you want, isn't it?"

"Yes, but . . ."

"Then it's what I want."

He held her close against him, loving her and wanting her to know it. His drifting years were behind him, the years which had belonged to the old fiddle-footed Kim Logan that Brit Bonham had not entirely trusted, a Kim Logan who had known only the transient values of life. The past was a turned page; the future was a clean white one ready to be written upon. They would write upon it together, Kim Logan and Rocky Avis.

Joseph Wayne was a pseudonym used by Wayne D. Overholser, an author who has won three Golden Spur awards from the Western Writers of America and who has a long list of fine Western titles to his credit. Overholser was born in Pomeroy, Washington, and attended the University of Montana, University of Oregon, and the University of Southern California before becoming a public school teacher and principal in various Oregon communities. He began writing for Western pulp magazines in 1936 and within a couple of years was a regular contributor to Street & Smith's *Western Story Magazine* and Fiction House's *Lariat Story Magazine*. *Buckaroo's Code* (1947) was his first Western novel and remains one of his best. In the 1950s and 1960s, having retired from academic work to concentrate on writing, he would publish as many as four books a year under his own name or a pseudonym, most prominently as Joseph Wayne. *The Violent Land* (1954), *The Lone Deputy* (1957), and *The Bitter Night* (1961) are among the finest of his early Overholser titles. Overholser's Western novels are based on a solid knowledge of the history and customs of the 19th-Century West, particularly when set in his two favorite Western states, Oregon and Colorado. Many of his novels are first person narratives, a technique that tends to bring an added dimension of vividness to the frontier experiences of his narrators and frequently, as in *Cast a Long Shadow* (1957), the female characters one encounters are among the most memorable. He has written his numerous novels with a consistent skill and an uncommon sensitivity to the depths of human character. Almost invariably, his stories weave a spell of their own with their scenes and images of social and economic forces often in conflict and the diverse ways of life and personalities that made the American Western frontier so unique a time and place in human history. *Nugget City* (1997) *Riders Of The Sundowns* (1997) and *Chumley's Gold* (1998) are his latest books.